THE
LIBERTY CIRCLE

Phil Campagna

Napoleon Publishing

Toronto, Ontario, Canada

Cover art: Christopher Chuckry

Published by Napoleon Publishing/RendezVous Press
Toronto, Ontario, Canada

Le Conseil des Arts du Canada   The Canada Council for the Arts
DEPUIS 1957   SINCE 1957

Napoleon Publishing gratefully acknowledges the support of the Canada Council for our publishing programme.

Printed in Canada

05 04 03 02 01 00   5 4 3 2 1

Canadian Cataloguing in Publication Data

Campagna, Phil, 1960-
    The liberty circle

ISBN 0-929141-69-5

I. Title.

PS8555.A525L52 2000   jC813'.54   C00-930313-8
PZ7.C35Li 2000

For my parents, who gave me an
environment I could learn in,
and for Jesse, reader Number One.

The author gratefully acknowledges the
assistance of Tina Tsallas and the
Great Titles Inc. literary agency.

One

The moment I walked into Captain Nemo's, I knew something was going on.

It wasn't so much a sight or a sound. You can't see anything in there until your eyes adjust, and there's always a lot of noise. It was more like an uneasy feeling, a sort of tension that filled the place. If anything, it was the *absence* of sound: the room was full, but everyone was whispering. Nervous.

Captain Nemo's was strange enough at the best of times. Entering it was like descending into the sea. The first thing that hit you was the colour: the carpet, the lights, even the windows facing the stairwell were an underwater aqua. The ceiling was a net, littered with glowing starfish. Weirdest of all were the aquariums, tucked into every nook and cranny. There were more tropical fish at Nemo's than in the average pet shop—but Captain Nemo's was an arcade.

"Corey!"

I peered through the gloom and saw Lisa waving to catch my attention. Beside her, my buddy Neil toiled at some video game, his eyes glowing like lasers behind the lenses of his glasses. I rounded a snooker table covered in blue and slid my arm round my girlfriend's waist. She was wearing her peace symbol earrings today, beneath an old-fashioned hat that nearly covered her short blonde hair.

She kissed me happily. "Your little friend here cheated," she said. "He won by psyching me out."

"That's how you play the game." I glanced around the room, my eyes adjusting at last. "What's going on here, anyway? This place seems weirder than usual."

"Weird is correct. It's those skinheads in the yellow Ts. They act like they own the place."

"They're here for a meeting or something," said Neil, not moving his eyes from the screen. "There's about a dozen of them in the back."

"They've even posted a guard," Lisa whispered. "That stupid-looking character in the hall."

I glanced at the entrance to the short hallway that led to the office at the back. An unwritten rule at Nemo's put that hallway strictly off-limits. Today that rule was being enforced by a surly-looking skinhead—not that you often saw any other kind.

The skins around here were the Brotherhood of Aryan Skinheads, BRASH or Brashboys for short. They looked pretty much like any other skinhead gang: shaved heads, combat boots, ridiculous tattoos, suspenders under leather bomber jackets. They looked like circus freaks, though you wouldn't tell them that to their faces. Most kids went out of their way to avoid them.

Having them around didn't exactly thrill me, but they'd never bothered me much—not me directly, that is. "So Gunnarsson's renting the room. So what?"

Lisa wrinkled her nose. "Did he have to rent it to

them? I hate those pigs. They're dangerous."

"They're in here more and more," Neil added nervously, still racking up the points. "I've never seen this many at once. They've been on Ranji's case since we got here."

I looked up at Ranji, the Pakistani guy who worked the counter. He was playing his guitar again. He did that sometimes when he was depressed about something. Lately, he'd been playing it a lot.

"Where is Gunnarsson, anyway?" I said. "I gotta ask him something."

"In the room with the pigs," Lisa replied. "Probably trying to keep them from trashing his office." She lowered her voice and looked toward the office with a sneer. "Why does he even let them in here? He can't be *that* desperate for business."

"They don't give him any," said Neil in a hushed voice. "I heard they get free tokens for the machines. He's organizing them."

"Gunnarsson?" I asked. "Organizing them for what?"

"He's getting them to clean up the park."

Lisa sniffed. "Oh, I'm sure. Skinheads with a social conscience."

"Fine. *Don't* believe me. I'm only here every day of the week."

"Okay," she argued, "so Peter Gunnarsson is a saint. I've seen him do all kinds of social work down here. But those guys are worthless trash."

"Nonetheless, they're cleaning the park. Want to give me a break from this thing?" Neil's game had finally ended. The top scores came on the screen, and his initials were in four different places.

I took over his machine, and he handed me a token. My mind wasn't on the game, though. I was thinking about Peter Gunnarsson. Lisa had a point: his hanging out with skinheads didn't make a lot of sense. It was kind of unnerving, having so many of them around. Like she'd said, they could be more than a little dangerous. Then again, if anyone on earth could reform the Brashboys, it would have to be the personable owner of Captain Nemo's.

Nobody knew all he'd done for me.

Like the pizza blast he'd thrown last year, for kids like me that hang out on the street too much. Nobody knew that Gunnarsson had been the only person in the world to sense something was wrong, the only person to ask. He'd taken me back to his office and made me talk and talk until I'd spilled the whole story. Until the tears had spilled from my eyes and I was telling him about—

The video screen went blank. In place of the game was this serious-looking blond guy with grey, dark-rimmed eyes: my own reflection.

"Damn it!" I swung around to where Keith Whynter and a bunch of his fellow skins leaned coolly against a wall. The meeting, apparently, had ended. "I ought to wrap that cord around your scrawny neck!"

"Oo-o-o-o!" Keith snarled. "Look out, guys, Corey's gonna whip us!"

He laughed, that moist, oily, skinhead laugh that set my teeth on edge. If a rat could laugh, I thought, that is what it would sound like. With his cream-coloured hair clipped short, the guy even looked like a rat—a tall, thin, pale one, raised in the dark like a roach. It was hard to believe we'd once hung out together.

A big, stupid-looking skin stepped away from the wall. He strolled toward Neil, taking the path of least resistance like all jerks do.

"Jew-boy," he growled. "Hey, there, Jew-boy."

What the—how had they found out about *that*? I sensed Neil tense up, anticipating a shove, and I stepped between them before it could happen. The skin was bigger than me, but I knew damn well I could take him if I had to. Him by himself, that is—except the Brashboys rarely worked alone.

"Whoa, lookit this." Another skin stepped forward. "This Corey must be a Jew-lover, Keith. Is that what it is, Corey? Is this the sort of company you keep?"

Behind him, Keith laughed again. "Jews are responsible for AIDS, Corey. Didn't you know that?"

"You wanna hassle someone?" I snarled. "Find someone who'll fight back."

The big skin grinned. "But we *like* passive resistors. We like kicking their pansy asses."

"You'll have to kick mine first."

Naturally, that set off a howl from the dorks at the wall. Behind the counter, alert at last, Ranji snapped to attention.

"Excuse me, please? What is going on there, please?"

"Shut up, paki," snapped a skin. "Go charm a snake."

In the moment that followed, there was a click from down the hall. I looked up to see Peter Gunnarsson strolling into the room. He was dressed casually as usual, in jeans and a golfing shirt. That ever-present smile tugged at the corners of his mouth. As always, though, everything about him told the world just exactly who was in charge.

I don't mean to say he walked around with an attitude. Peter Gunnarsson was genuinely easy to like. He was friendly, easy-going, and he talked to you on the level. It didn't matter if you were eight or eighty, he'd always make like you were his equal. That, and the shock of blond over his forehead, made him seem a whole lot younger than thirty-eight.

He had this thing, though—this sort of hardness in his eyes. Like maybe he wouldn't be so nice if you tried screwing around with the rules.

That hardness was there right now as he gazed at the skinhead in front of me. "Chet? Is there a problem here?" An eyebrow lifted ever so slightly.

The skin looked sullen as he shuffled back to his friends. "No," he said, "sir."

Gunnarsson pulled an envelope from his pocket and handed it to Chet. "Take this to Palmer, would you? And tell him I need to see him the second he gets a chance." Quietly, he added, "We haven't got a lot of time."

Chet nodded and left, without so much as a word of lip. Gunnarsson looked about at the others. "Okay, fellas—you all have your assignments. Head on over to the park. I'll join you in a bit."

And in front of my eyes, they did exactly what they were told. Surreal! The Brashboys were social parasites, and Gunnarsson had them acting like nuns. I glanced at Neil, expecting the smug expression he usually wore when proven right. All I saw this time was a look of total terror.

"Corey! Long time no see, old chum. How've you been?" Gunnarsson came over to where we still stood by Neil's game. "Hello, Lisa. Good to have you back. Did you come to water Neil? He's here so much, we've begun to suspect he's a potted plant."

"Mr. G.," I said, "I gotta ask you something."

"Shoot."

"That poster...the one for Camp Liberty. How does a guy get in?" I indicated the neon sheet pinned to the wall behind him.

I'd seen them posted all over the Flats. The top part was a photo, broken into lines for effect, of a guy and a girl paddling a canoe. Lily pads spotted the water around them, and trees on a distant shore were mirrored in the lake. "FREE YOURSELF AT CAMP LIBERTY" urged a caption underneath. And beneath that:

LEARN TO LIVE, NOW!

Are you bored with life? Uncertain of the future? Dissatisfied with the world? Do you want to do something now to help your country, your fellow man, yourself?

Then come to CAMP LIBERTY, ten acres of paradise on the shores of Liberty Lake. You will learn about the way things are—and how they can be—in the most intensive three weeks of living you will ever experience.

Make no mistake—Camp Liberty is not a school. In fact, we can guarantee non-stop action from the moment you arrive. You can swim, play tennis, go hiking, horseback riding, canoeing—the list is endless. And you will undergo a learning experience that will benefit you the rest of your life.

Interested? Contact Peter Gunnarsson
at Captain Nemo Entertainment.

For maybe five long seconds, Gunnarsson stared at me in silence. You'd have thought I'd belched in church.

Then his eyes rolled up to the ceiling, where they focused on a purple starfish. He reached through the net to adjust it. "I think," he said, "that all our spaces have been filled."

"You think? I mean...I thought you were organizing it yourself. Your name is on the poster."

"It is, isn't it?" He glanced at Lisa and Neil, then turned a thoughtful gaze on me. "How old are you, exactly?"

"Sixteen."

"Uh-huh. And how are things going these days? At home, I mean. How's Marty?"

I flushed, wishing he hadn't brought that up in front of Lisa and Neil. "Things are okay," I told him, and that was a lie. They were better, all right, but still far from being okay. "I don't know about Marty. We haven't heard from him for months."

Gunnarsson nodded. "It's been a while since I've asked, I know. I've been...rather busy with things, thanks to my dear sweet ex-wife. But you remember what I told you? About what to do if it gets too bad, and you've nowhere else to go?"

"Yeah, I remember. Thanks."

It was one more reason to like the guy. He had offered more than once to put me up when things got crazy. Most of those times, though, I'd wound up staying at Neil's. His mom didn't mind, or at least said she didn't. Once, when I got sick of mooching off them, I just stayed out and slept in the park. It's not too much fun, sleeping in the park.

"Just remember," Gunnarsson said, "the offer still stands."

"Thanks."

He gave me a friendly punch on the shoulder—then strode back toward his office.

I ran into the hallway after him. "Mr. G.? About the camp?"

He winced. "Oh, yes. All right. I'll get you an application." He went down the hall to his office.

He emerged a minute later, locking the door behind him. He handed me a form about ten pages thick. "I can't make any promises," he said, "but fill this out and I'll see what I can do. And now, if you'll excuse me, I've got some litter to pick."

I gave him my best look of disbelief. "You haven't actually got skinheads doing that, have you?"

Gunnarsson smiled. "I actually have, yes. Getting people to do things is a trick I learned years ago. You remember, those stories I told you about my days in the Moony cult?"

"Well—" I stopped, choosing my words carefully. Gunnarsson was just about the last person in the world I wanted to offend—but some things just needed saying.

"Can you trust them, though? I mean, I'm not putting them down or anything, it's just that skinheads are sort of, well, evil."

His smile faded, and just a trace of that hardness returned to his eyes. "Evil. Well, I'm glad you decided not to put them down." He sighed, and shook his head. "Look. There's a lot of problems down here, out on the streets. You should know that as well as anyone. Well, I'm running a business here. And if there's problems, I have to fix them, or there won't be a business to run. Who'd want to come to an arcade surrounded by broken neighbourhoods, horrible crime? I'm trying to do something here, trying to patch my one small corner of the world. That's all."

He looked about as close to angry as I'd ever seen him before, and it practically made me cringe. "Sorry," I gushed. "I didn't mean to put them down. I—"

Unexpectedly, he broke into a smile. "Don't worry about it," he said. "Just don't go knocking what you don't understand. Skinheads are angry young people, Corey, but maybe they've got their reasons. All they need is direction, a place to put that anger. They have many interesting ideas, you know." He laughed dryly. "For that matter, so did the Moonies."

He left the arcade then, and I returned to Lisa and Neil, a bit discombobulated.

"Got it," I said. "I never thought—I should have got copies for you two!"

"Forget that," said Neil, fishing in his pocket for video tokens. He found one, looked nervously about, and put it back in his pocket. I swear, the guy was shaking like a pneumatic drill. "I wouldn't want to go there anyway."

"Why not?"

He shrugged. "I've heard bad things about it. Like it's a camp for people who think they're better than everyone else."

"So what? We've all got to be better than someone."

"That's how those skinheads think."

I swore. "Come on. You're just sore at them for giving you such a hard time. They're lucky they travel in packs. If I ever catch one of them alone..."

"That wouldn't solve anything."

That figured—they'd just insulted his religion, and all he could do was be passive about it. But that's the kind of person Neil Haymond was. He'd give you the shirt off his back, even if you'd stolen his pants. I don't mean that he was a wimp; Neil was hardly that. He just didn't believe in scrapping.

The guy was Barney Rubble.

"Come on," I said, turning for the door. "Let's get out of here before those guys come back and Lisa lectures them on 'social conscience'." Lisa was big on social conscience. She was one of the few people I'd met from Harrington Gardens who was. Like a lot of rich people, she didn't really understand what it was like to live in this part of town. But she tried.

"*Ssst!*" A sound from the counter stopped me.

I walked back over to Ranji. He had set aside his guitar and now leaned against the counter with shadowed eyes. "What's up, old buddy?" I asked.

He glanced carefully about before answering. He seemed awfully pale, I thought, a pretty neat trick for a

Pakistani. "You asked," he whispered, "about that camp in the poster?"

"Yeah. What about it?"

"Listen to me, my friend—and pay very close attention. Do not, Corey, do not do anything with that camp. It is full of, of..." He gestured with his hand, as if groping for the right words. "Full of bad things, wrong things, evil. Do not go there, my friend, not for anything. You will wish you had not, I am telling you."

I laughed nervously, half-thinking that this was a joke. "Why, does the devil live there or something?"

Ranji nodded. "Yes. Almost. I do not know if there is a devil in this world, but if there is, he must live there. I—" He broke off all of a sudden, gazing at something behind me.

I turned around, but whoever it was had already slunk back into the depths of Captain Nemo's. When I turned back to Ranji, he was busily wiping the counter. Several seconds went by before he spoke again.

"Look...I cannot tell you all that I know. If I did, Mr. Gunnarsson would fire me. It is that simple. But I am telling you this, Corey: stay away from Camp Liberty!" He paused for a moment, maybe wondering whether I believed him. When he spoke again, it was little more than a whisper. "You see it here, today," he said. "Those ones who shave their heads. They would have hurt your friend. Well, there is evil worse than that..."

I shook my head, just a bit annoyed. It had suddenly occurred to me that an afternoon with the skinheads might have done something to warp Ranji's views. "Look—a lot of those guys live in this part of town. Of course they're going to hang out here. If it bothers you so much, why don't you get another job?"

Ranji shook his head. "I live above this place," he whispered. "It costs little. My wife, she is having a child soon. And—" He stopped suddenly and looked at me funny. Like he was really lonely all of a sudden, like he needed someone to talk to. And all he had at that moment, maybe at any moment, was a sixteen-year-old kid in an arcade. "She is not come to this country the proper way."

"Aw, geez." I backed away from the counter, more than a bit uncomfortable. "You shouldn't be telling me all this, you know? What if Gunnarsson found out?"

He looked at me stonily. "Mr. Gunnarsson knows," he said flatly.

I turned and looked for an escape, anything to get me away from Too Much Information. I spotted Lisa gesturing at the door—rich, lovely Lisa, whose status in life dictated that she never wait for anything. I loved her anyway.

"Look...I gotta go." I backed away to the door.

Coming out of Captain Nemo's is like emerging from the sea: the heat and sunlight hit you like a truck, especially in mid-afternoon. For the longest time after you leave, everything is an ugly shade of yellow. We stood there on the walk, blinking in the light, while I fished about for my shades.

An old woman hobbled by against the flow of pedestrians, tightly clutching a tiny purse. She must have been one of the first, I thought, one who'd lived here for years. One who couldn't afford to leave now that the neighbourhood had rotted away.

"Hey! Grandma!" A couple of skins lounged in front of the drug store, taunting passers-by.

"Grandma" ignored them. I watched her work her way past the winos, drug lords and freaks, hell-bent on getting through them alive. I suddenly felt kind of depressed.

"This neighbourhood sucks," I muttered.

Lisa nodded. "And Mr. Gunnarsson isn't helping." She pulled her hat off in the heat. "Why's he letting skinheads into Nemo's? He's going to wreck the place."

"How come you worry so much about what goes on down here?"

"How come you don't?" She gave me that look, that Greenpeace—Amnesty International—warpath look. "Those skins could've hurt Neil bad, and you don't even seem to care. I swear you never read the papers. Do you know what's happening down here?"

I nearly squawked out loud. "Do I know what's happening? Are you kidding? Besides, they might not have done anything bad."

"Right, I forgot. You used to hang out with them."

"*Some* of them," I corrected. "And that's completely in the past."

"Whatever. Sometimes I'm not so sure. You've got to believe it though—those skins are a growing menace, and the cops don't even take them seriously."

I sighed and glanced at Neil. "Listen to her. The expert."

Neil hitched his glasses up on his nose and looked across at the skins. He reminded me of a nearsighted chipmunk. "She's right," he said quietly. "Some days I think I don't want to come down here anymore. It's getting worse."

"They're really a menace when they swarm," Lisa added. "They pick out someone on the street and gang up on them. They're like killer bees."

"I know," I replied. "I live here, remember? Anyhow, they mostly just go for minorities. Blacks. Sikhs. Gays. Punks, especially. They love punks." Punks dressed differently from skinheads. They usually had different views from them, too. Punks and skinheads did not get along, and gang fights were pretty common. A kid had been killed last year.

"They found out I'm Jewish," said Neil, a quaver in his voice.

"You should have been okay," I told him. "What'd you do, wear your beanie in public?"

Neil gave me a withering look. "Yarmulke."

"Your mamma," I retorted.

That got him smiling again.

We started off for his place, the afternoon traffic pounding all around. We hadn't gone three blocks before our bodies were sticky with sweat. It would probably still be hot when the daytime people left and the night-time people emerged. I felt cold anyway and even shivered when a bead of perspiration ran down my back. Ranji's warning was back in my head.

Do not go there, my friend, not for anything. Stay away from Camp Liberty!

Two

It was cool in Neil's room in the basement, and there was a sink by the stairs where we could wash the city's filth from our faces. Down here, the street was reduced to a muted roar, a muffled drone like starship engines. I lay back against the bed with my arms around Lisa, staring at wonders on the ceiling. Neil was explaining his latest creation.

"It's the solar system," he declared. "Each one of those spheres is a different planet. That little blue one there is Earth, and the sun is the ceiling light."

"What are those loops they're mounted on?" I asked. "Do they show the planets' routes?"

"My friends," he announced grandly, "they do much more than that." He stood and flipped the light switch, and an electric motor hummed to life. "Ta-dum!"

The planets were moving in their orbits. Some flipped round the "sun" in a second, while others took more than a minute. One had a distinctly lopsided route—I think that was supposed to be Pluto. I shook my head. "This must have taken you weeks!"

Neil beamed. "It did. I used parts of an old ceiling fan. The problem was getting the planets to move at just the right speeds." He frowned. "If only I could figure out a way to make them spin on their axes."

I looked at Lisa, who gazed back with a knowing smile. Our friend's mind spun on an axis of its own, never resting a moment. This wasn't his first such amazing project. He'd built a working robot once, out of a discarded vacuum cleaner. A length of pipe from an empty lot had become a telescope. And every year he created an incredible light display for Christmas—or rather, for Chanukah. It slowed the traffic on his street.

He put on one of our favourite tapes and sat back to stare at his universe. I closed my eyes, wondering just how many hours the three of us had spent like this. Captain Nemo's aside, Neil's room was the only spot I ever felt comfortable with Lisa. My place was out of the question. But it had to be somewhere in this part of town. As long as we were in the Flats, I didn't have to worry about how shabby my clothes looked. Or what my dad did for a living. Or the embarrassing fact that I sometimes went a bit hungry.

When I visited Lisa in Harrington Gardens, things were quite a bit different.

I squeezed her shoulders gently, thinking about it. "What does your Dad think of you hanging out with us white trash?"

She looked at me with an odd expression. "He doesn't mind. He likes you guys, and besides, he trusts me. Mom's the one you have to worry about. Anyhow, it's my life—I can associate with whatever trash I wish."

"Thanks," I said. "I think."

"Besides..." She snuggled against me and gave me a

little hug. "You won't always be here, will you? You'll get out of this neighbourhood someday."

Just for a moment, I felt an angry warmth spread through my cheeks. Who did she think she was, anyway, putting down the Flats? It wasn't a crime to live here. But she hadn't meant it that way—and anyhow, I hoped she was right.

"No," I said at last. "I won't always live here."

"You're going to be an *artiste*."

"Damn straight I am. In fact..."

I got up and went to the easel in the corner. Neil let me keep it in his room, since I practically lived there anyway. I turned on the battered clip-on light, and the rest of the world disappeared. *I* disappeared, that is— when I'm puzzling over a painting, I'm oblivious to everything. And this one was more of a puzzle than most.

I had Lisa standing on a downtown street in one of her designer outfits, arms lightly crossed at her waist. She gazed from the paint with a fragile innocence she only rarely showed in life. I had her illuminated, like on a summer afternoon, though the background was clearly at night. Neon signs glowed warm behind her.

It was the background, I decided. The background wasn't right. The portrait was nearly finished, but it needed something else. It had the effect I wanted: innocence in the midst of reality. But the background...

The background was too real, too commonplace, too plain. It needed a touch of strangeness. It needed a bit of magic, like...like that sparkle in Neil's eyes when he'd explained his solar system...

I must have reached for the paints, because suddenly

a brush was in my hand. Titanium white, Grumbacher red, Mars black oozed onto the palette. Then my hands began to move, and I just stood and watched what they did. That's the way it works for me—it's like somebody else takes over. Streaks of colour flew onto the canvas board, mostly red and white. Hints of others joined in: yellow ochre, cerulean blue, pale green. Amber, lots of that. They mixed, and they blended, and when there was almost enough, they stopped. And then Indian, Neil's beloved old Irish setter, nudged my leg. I popped awake and stared at the finished painting.

"Will you look at that?" I said to Lisa. "Two weeks before your birthday."

It was a time-lapse version of what I'd had before, with streaks of light showing the paths the cars had taken. The people, too, were blurred, on the sidewalk behind Lisa. It looked like something out of *National Geographic*. And it looked good.

Lisa stared in awe. "It's beautiful," she whispered, and her eyes looked kind of moist.

"That's pretty awesome," Neil agreed.

I smiled and took my brushes out to the sink to clean them. I'd started the painting for Lisa as a gift for her sixteenth birthday. I wasn't rich like her, but I could give her something nice just the same.

When I walked back into Neil's room, she was still staring at her portrait. "Corey," she asked suddenly, "has your dad changed his mind yet, about you going to college?"

"Naw," I admitted. "And I'm not gonna hold my breath. He still figures I should finish school next year and go out and get a job. We need the cash at home."

"Oh, Corey..." She looked at me with genuine sadness. "I really, really hope you get to go. It means so much to me. It's easier for me, I guess—I practically get what I want on a platter. But you..."

She didn't need to finish; I could tell what she meant to say. *But you have to try so hard, fight so much, just to get what others take for granted.* Well, big deal. If I had to try twice as hard to get what others had, I'd try four times as hard instead. I would get control of my life.

But I didn't tell her that. "There's that scholarship," I said instead. "I'm going to get it, too—at least, I'm pretty sure." I gave a careless stretch and a yawn, as if it didn't matter. As if going to college and studying art and becoming the painter I knew I could be wasn't the very reason I breathed.

I needed a subject to change to, so I picked up my Camp Liberty application. I spread it out on the floor, and the three of us looked it over.

CAMP LIBERTY

is not an ordinary summer camp. It was designed by the leaders of today—educators, politicians, religious leaders and idealists from many fields—to meet the needs of tomorrow's leaders. It is, without apology, an elitist camp. You would not be reading this form if one of our administrators had not recognized you as a member of that elite.

For a moment, that stopped me cold. "*Elitist?* Hey, Neil, is that what you meant when you said it was a camp for people who think they're better than everyone else?"

Neil chuckled. "So what makes you elite?"

The application rambled on about all the great things you could do at Camp Liberty. Then the questions came. They started out with the usual, like name, age, address, family doctor and so on. Then they got kind of weird:

> Read over the following questions carefully. Place a checkmark by the answer(s) of your choice. Try to be honest, as the acceptance of your application does not depend on your answers. We only want to get your views on various subjects so that we have a picture of who you are. Your opinions will be respected. We will not try to change you.

"Various" was right. They asked about everything, from what I knew about politics to what my favourite colour was. Some of the questions were stranger than others. One asked if I thought a conspiracy was trying to take over the world. Another wanted to know if I thought it was wrong for people of different races to marry. And one asked if I thought people of certain races were inferior in intelligence. I answered that with a "yes"—that's just how I felt back then.

Lisa went straight up. "I knew it! I just knew it! Corey, you're a bigot!"

I flushed. "I'm not," I said. "It's just the way I feel."

"You've got no social conscience at all. None. No wonder you didn't want to volunteer with me at that street mission Mom helped finance. Corey, you live in the Flats! How can you be this way?"

"I didn't want to help," I reminded, "because your friends in Harrington Gardens don't even know what the problems are. That mission won't fix anything."

"Kids," said Neil. "No fighting."

Lisa shook her head. "What is it with these questions, anyway?"

"They just want to know how we think."

"Yeah, but...a conspiracy taking over the world?"

"They just want to know how we think."

She shook her head. "Be careful, Corey. You know the way you are."

I blinked and looked at Neil. He just grinned and rolled his eyes. Even the dog seemed to smile.

"'The way I am?' Excuse me?"

Lisa furrowed her brow. "It's like...you know when you hung out with that Keith guy?"

"Don't remind me."

"You had your hair cropped. You wanted to be a skinhead."

"I did not!"

"You did, Corey," she insisted. "You always do—every time something new comes along, you want to join up, sign in, be a part of it. Sometimes you look before you leap. But sometimes it's, like, you're too trusting? You want so much to be a part you forget to question till it's too late."

I sighed and shook my head. Best just to let this one slide, I thought. Anyhow, she might be right. I had sort of got sucked in a little with Keith and his friends. Once. Temporarily.

But they'd blown it when they'd picked on Neil.

I read over the final paragraph of my application, the one about money. Three weeks of fun, it said, would cost three hundred dollars—or one-fifty for 'unemployed'. That wasn't a problem, I guessed. I had nearly seven hundred dollars in the bank. It had taken three years to save that much, walking dogs, shovelling snow, helping out at a fast food joint. It was supposed to be for college. But three weeks! I could get away from myself for a while, do some serious planning. Maybe I could figure out how to deal with those problems that had been eating my life.

Problems like my screwed-up family.

We hung round Neil's until six, when Mrs. Haymond came down the stairs. It was Chinese food for supper, she announced, and would Lisa and I like to stay? But Lisa had already called home for a ride, and I said I was needed at home. See, besides Neil, there was his little sister Hannah to support—not to mention Indian—and Mrs. H. had to do it alone. Anyway, I decided, I shouldn't need charity just to stay fed. They'd given me plenty of that already.

I went out and waited with Lisa until her mother's car came gliding toward us. It was a Mercedes, loaded, and it looked comically out of place. Lisa offered me a ride as usual, and as usual, I turned it down. She'd probably laugh if I told her why. But I couldn't go from her world to the world of my home that fast. I needed a break in between, and walking gave me that. Especially in this neighbourhood.

I turned off Neil's shabby street and on to one that wasn't so nice. Neon signs flickered here like heat lightning: CHEQUES CASHED, BAIL BONDS 24 HOURS, XXX MOVIES. The ladies of the night were already out, strutting their stuff on the walks. With sidelong glances they watched the cars, the ones circling the block like slow, metallic sharks. I'd always thought they were pretty pathetic, those guys in the cars.

A block off the main strip was a street of grungy, grate-windowed shops. Behind that was a space, a big, littered lot where a factory once had stood. I walked through it carefully, headed for a dismal area of run-down apartment blocks. Mine was third from the right.

I stopped. There was a car in our space, but not Dad's old Ford. A blue Civic with out-of-province plates. I remembered the last time someone had parked in Dad's spot, nearly four months ago. He'd come home in a rotten mood to begin with, and that one little incident had sent him over the edge. It was the night Marty had left.

With a sigh, I headed up to our third-floor suite.

When I opened the door, a wild-looking redhead with amazingly tight jeans was standing on the other side. When she saw me, she let out a shriek. I'd never seen her before in my life.

"My God!" she gushed, peering over a set of yellow shades. "Marty never told me you were such a looker!"

Marty. That explained everything. He must have latched onto this genius, at least four years his senior, to get a lift home from wherever. Next he'd be telling us how they were going to get married as soon as he settled into his latest career.

And there he was now, his dark, curly head poked round the corner from the kitchen. "*Corey!*" he roared, and he bounded into the hall. In an instant he was all over me, squeezing me like a roll of wipe. "How's it goin', little brother?"

"Hello, Marty," I replied, pulling back a little. Already I could smell the familiar stench of beer and nicotine.

Marty grinned and threw an arm around Red's waist. "This is Corey, the li'l brother I told you about. And this, Corey—" He let his hand slip below her waist. "This heah's a li'l sumthin' ah picked up at a ranch in th' mountains. Name's Valerie. Pardy li'l thang, ain't she?"

Valerie giggled and slapped his hand away, but didn't seem to mind when he put it back. She looked me over for several seconds. "He looks a lot like you," she said.

I just stood and stared at the two of them. They must have been matched in heaven.

"Nice meeting you," I said at last. "I have to get cleaned up." Without waiting for a reply, I stepped into the john off the hall. I turned on the water in the sink, full blast.

I stood working the suds through my fingers, the steam rising to my face. It wasn't right. Things were going badly enough as it was. It wasn't right he should show up now. I stopped and stared at my hands. They were shaking, and no wonder. Marty was going to ruin everything.

"Hey, Cor."

I started, and looked up at my brother. He'd been standing in the doorway watching.

"You don't seem happy to see me," he said.

"Should I be?"

He shrugged. "Maybe not." He traced his finger along the edge of the door, then let out a dry laugh. "I guess I really caused a scene when I was here last, huh?"

"I guess that you did."

"I really upset old Mom."

"You knocked her off the wagon."

"Dad wanted to kill me."

"So did I." I shut off the taps with a force that made the pipes bang. "Why'd you come back?"

He looked startled. "I live here."

"Really? Last time you left, you swore you'd never be back."

"Oh, that." He put on a lopsided grin. "I went to Banff for a while, out in the Rocky Mountains. I was working at a resort. You'd have liked it, Cor. Women there you wouldn't believe." He made a gesture with his hands, indicating boobs the size of melons.

"Thanks. I've got all the women I need."

"Yeah? You still seeing Lisa?"

"Still." I brushed past him to get out of the john, but he caught my arm. He'd slapped on his sorry look now, the one he always wore when he was about to apologize for something.

This time, though, he wasn't apologizing. "Corey," he said, "do you think I should have come back?"

That floored me. Marty never, I mean never, talked serious about anything—especially if it involved himself. And now he'd asked me this, and I could tell from the look in his eyes how badly he needed an answer. I thought of what had happened before he left, what had happened since, and what was probably going to happen now that he was back. It wasn't too hard to give him an answer.

"No. You shouldn't have."

He turned away a little and blinked. I could tell I'd hurt him, but he'd wanted the truth. And there was more: "Things got worse after you showed up last. Dad got laid off, and he and Mom fight constantly. I can't sleep or study when they do that, but I've got nowhere else to live. Some nights I've stayed over at Neil's, or just slept out in the park. The only good things are that Mom's stopped drinking, and I haven't had you around to screw up my life!" My voice cracked like a little kid's, too much emotion coming up my throat.

Marty looked at me blankly. "You slept in the park?"

I spun away and left the bathroom, determined not to say anything else.

His voice called after me: "Why didn't I know about this?"

"Because," I shot back, "you're never here. And even when you are, you're too pissed out of your skull to know." I reached the kitchen door with my eyes stinging. Sixteen years old, and I was on the verge of bawling like a baby.

"Corey? Is that you?" Mom called to me from the stove.

"No," I said bitterly. "It's someone else."

"Come here for a minute, honey. I want you to try something."

Honey? She hadn't called me that in ages. I went to the stove and she held out a spoonful of sauce.

"Taste it," she said, and she actually smiled as she said it. "It's a variation on my old spaghetti sauce."

I tried it, and it was delicious. It had been a long time.

"I decided to make something special tonight," she said. "For Marty and his girl."

There it was. *For Marty*. I'd had my appendix out the year before and had been in the hospital two weeks with complications. The night I came home, we'd had canned soup. But then, I wasn't Marty. I wasn't the one who took after her.

At supper, Mom asked Valerie to tell us all about herself. She was only too happy to do that. She came from a farm in Alberta, where her parents were drilling for oil. As soon as they found some, they would all be rich, and she'd trade her Civic for a BMW. Dad kept pretty quiet for most of the meal, as he had since he'd got laid off. He asked only the one question—just to be polite, I guess:

"Does your family keep poultry on the farm?"

"Poultry? That's like chickens and roosters and stuff, right?" Valerie giggled. "No-o-o-o. They're too smelly, and they mess all over the yard. We have a dog, though. His name is Bart."

"I see." After that, Mom got to ask all the questions.

We made it almost all the way through supper, but I knew it wouldn't last. I could see it coming a block away. Dad had shoved the last bit of food in his mouth and leaned away from the table.

"Think I'll hit the sack," he muttered. "I got that temporary in the morning. Might lead to full-time if I'm really quick on my feet."

"We'll be quiet, then," said Marty, "when we go to bed."

There was a click as Dad set down his fork. "What exactly do you mean by that?" he asked, wiping his mouth on his sleeve.

"When we go to bed," Marty said, "we'll be quiet. The

sofa bed's in the living room, right outside your door."

Dad's cheek bulged out from where he stuck his tongue. He glared across the table at Mom, who suddenly looked very tired.

"I don't see what difference it could possibly make now," she said quietly.

"'Course you don't," Dad shot back. "No one in your family would." He turned back to Marty and was about to start in when Marty cut him off.

"You don't expect us to stay in a motel, do you?"

"Don't be stupid. But there's a spare cot in the closet we could haul out for Valerie. She can sleep on that."

Marty's face grew red. "I pay rent here."

"Seventy-five bucks a month, *when* you're here. For *single* occupancy."

"Fine!" Marty dug out his wallet. "I'll give you one-fifty for this month, how's that?"

"I think you've missed the point, smart-ass..."

"What difference could it possibly make?" Mom asked, her voice beginning to rise.

"Florence, you stay out of this. If you're going to defend this kid every time he opens his smart mouth..."

I got up and left the table. It grew louder as I left the kitchen, louder still as I locked myself into my room. They'd already switched to other subjects, old hurts dragged out of the closet to be put through another round. I plugged my headphones into my ghetto-blaster and cranked the volume to the max. To hell with all of them. I lay back on my bed, dreading the spaces between songs, when I could hear the battle raging. Dreading the pounding on my door that would tell me Dad had noticed my absence.

Maybe you know how it is. You're living in someone else's space, and they make all the rules. They decide when and what you eat, when you have to keep the noise down at night, maybe even what you wear. You're not allowed freedom of travel. Every little thing you do causes someone to object. You're yelled at all the time, for not doing things they want you to, and for doing things they don't.

And other things, like arguments and fights that don't even involve you, but that still mess up your mind. Sometimes it gets so bad you only want to leave, to go somewhere and clear your mind. But the law doesn't allow it, because you're underage. You don't have a car, or maybe even a licence, and besides, you still have to be in at a certain time.

You're jammed in between, with no way out: you know you're too old to be living by the rules of others, but they won't let you live on your own. Living alone seems impossible, anyway; there's that many things no one's taught you yet. But you can't take it at home anymore. Some days you feel you'll explode, that your mind will change somehow under the strain, and you'll forget the kind of person you wanted to be.

That's how I was feeling that night. And sometime during the blackest part of that night, I vowed to make it to Camp Liberty. And to hell with Ranji and his gloom-and-doom warnings.

Three

City Parking Lot #17 was a scene of organized panic. A turquoise bus perched in the corner, the word "Liberty" in its destination slot. Beside it lay a mountain of gear. T-shirted camp officials worked frantically to load it all, each with an eye on the sky. Purple clouds were congregating above, their bellies rumbling with thunder.

I stood waiting with the other campers, brooding along with the weather. It perfectly matched my mood.

"Don't be so growlish," said Lisa at my elbow. "I won't see you again for weeks."

"It just makes me feel like such a puppy," I said. "I must be the youngest one here."

"C'mon, there's a few our age. Five or six of the guys."

"They all look like skids. Like they come from broken homes." A thought struck me and I laughed dryly. "Maybe this is charity. Maybe Gunnarsson's taking a few underage kids, but only if we're bashed-up models from the child abuse lot."

Lisa gasped. "Don't even think that way."

"Why not? I'd qualify."

"You're feeling sorry for yourself."

"Yeah. Maybe." I turned and put my arm around her.

"I still don't see why you didn't try to get in. We could have had a blast."

"I told you—Dad's taking us to Montreal. Besides, I didn't want to fight with him. Not after *that*." She nodded toward the red VW bug parked neatly under a tree. No kidding at all, it was a gift for her sixteenth birthday.

"No," I replied, "I guess you wouldn't want to annoy him now. Life must be rough when you're rich."

"That's not funny."

"Sorry."

"Everybody aboard that's going aboard," shouted Gunnarsson. "Liberty awaits!"

I turned to Lisa and kissed her. "Promise you'll be good? Three weeks is a long time."

She gave me a pitying look. "How much trouble could I get into? I'll be with my family!"

"I'll write you anyway. Maybe even while I'm on the bus. I'll mail it when they stop for gas."

That made her smile. "Don't be an idiot."

"You're right. I'll phone when they stop for gas."

She laughed and kissed me again. I felt a drop of rain on my back.

"All right, Corey." Mr. Gunnarsson leaned out the door of the bus. "You can do your mating when you return."

A wave of laughter swept through the bus, and I turned and got myself on. The guy I sat beside was grinning like a jack-o-lantern.

A gust of wind rose as we pulled from the lot, and water splattered against the windows. I looked out and saw Lisa standing there alone, waving goodbye in the rain. She looked lonely, somehow, and vulnerable. Despite the VW bug.

"You turn the nicest shade of red when you're embarrassed," the guy beside me observed.

I turned toward my seatmate. Like most of the others, he was older than me, around twenty or twenty-one. He sported wire-frame glasses, one of those goofy goatee beards, and red hair which he wore in a ponytail.

He stuck out his hand. "Yannick Quisell's the name," he said. "But don't let me bore you with *my* problems."

"I'm Corey Copeland."

"Ah." He stroked that tiny beard. "Interesting."

"Why's that?"

"Copeland. It's English. Everyone on this bus seems to be that, or Scandinavian, or Germanic...white peoples. There are no ethnic groups represented here, though I personally know of two blacks who applied."

"Maybe," said a familiar voice behind us, "whoever handled the applications was smart enough to reject theirs."

We turned to find Keith Whynter slouched in the seat behind us, smiling his milky smile. Another skinhead sat beside him, a short little runt with traces of moustache— another of the jerks who'd been harassing Neil. I hadn't seen either of them when I'd stepped onto the bus, or I'd have chosen a different seat.

Great, I thought, Brashboys coming to camp. Getting away from them was a small part of the reason I'd wanted to go in the first place. I could tell this was going to be a really fun vacation.

It got me started on the trip riding a wave of self-pity.

I needed this time away. I couldn't have any distractions. I had to format my life, plan what I wanted to do, decide how I wanted to live. I'd just had two and a half weeks of Marty, and I needed some time to relax.

Not that things at home had fallen apart just yet. The fight on the first night had been the last, and Valerie now slept where she wanted. But it was an uneasy truce. We were all being so nice to each other, it was nerve-wracking. It was a peace that couldn't last.

I looked out the window. We'd left the city soaking behind us and were on the freeway through the suburbs. I felt lonely all of a sudden, depressed, like I was leaving something behind. Lisa, maybe. Feelings change fast when you're sixteen, and three weeks was a very long time.

Five hours later, we were still on the road.

In the bus, the glow of reading lamps made a homey, cocoon sort of feeling. A few passengers dozed in their seats. I willed myself to do the same, but my eyes kept returning to the window. The scenery gave me the creeps.

The bus had taken several turns, the freeway dwindling with each. We were on a narrow, gravelled road now, winding through wilderness. There were no high-rises here, no houses, only a thickening wall of forest. So much space, I thought, with hardly anyone in it. Could people actually live here?

Above, the clouds had become an endless blanket of grey. The silhouettes of jack pines had begun to look like sentries, dark soldiers flanking the road to make sure we stayed on track.

"ATTENTION, CAMPERS..."

A dozen or so campers got jolted rudely awake. At the front of the bus stood Peter Gunnarsson, microphone in hand. He leaned to turn down an amplifier.

"Sorry about that," he said. "If you look out your windows right now, you'll see we are well into the northern woods. Just a short distance from the highway lies virgin forest."

"Wonder how it got its name?" muttered Yannick, stirring beside me.

"In a few minutes, ladies and gentlemen, we'll arrive at Camp Liberty!"

A mild cheer went up, from people who only wanted to sleep.

Gunnarsson smiled and shook his head. "That's not the kind of enthusiasm I'm looking for! What you're about to enter is not your average summer camp. You ought to know that by now." He paused for a moment, and when he spoke again, his voice was heavy and low: "Camp Liberty is an experiment, the seed of something great. A dozen or more professionals came together to make it work. And it's designed to change your lives—the country—maybe even the world! I don't know if it's possible to describe the experience before the fact. You'll have to be there, for a few days in fact, before you begin to understand. But I'd like you to have some idea of our goals. *Your* goals."

With that, he began his first speech. I have to admit, it was quite a speech. His voice started low, then rose like a preacher's until it rang through the bus like gunfire. By then we were wide awake and listening to every word.

He told us we were living in danger, every minute of our lives. He told us we shouldn't have to. He spoke of a common enemy, the force causing all this danger. He didn't really get into who or what it was, but I think we each had our own ideas. At the camp, he promised, we'd tackle these problems head-on. We'd crush them.

"And now," he announced when he was done, "there's someone I'd like you to meet."

A slim young woman seated near the front got up and took his place. She was about twenty, I guess, with long blonde hair and a yellow Camp Liberty T-shirt. Some of the guys whistled enthusiastically; she wore that T-shirt really well. She flashed us a toothpaste smile.

"Thank you," she said, and even her voice was cute. "My name is Julie, and I've been asked to work up a little spirit in you guys for the final stretch of our journey. There are already some campers at Camp Liberty. When we arrive, let's show them they're in for some competition! And the best way to do that is to sing! Let's all start in right now:

This land is your land,

This land is my land..."

She started in, all right, but for several painful seconds, it looked like it'd be a solo. She kept at it, though, not blushing or anything, and pretty soon a few joined in. Before you knew it, everyone on the bus was making a fool of themselves. Even I joined in after a while.

The bus slowed, then turned onto an almost hidden road. Branches brushed at the windows, and I could feel us bogging down in the mud. Still they rallied us to sing; Gunnarsson went up and down the aisle shouting out the words as Julie picked up the tempo.

"From the Arctic Circle,
To the Great Lakes waters..."

We lurched through a gap in a chain link fence and manoeuvred a twisted turn. Finally, just as the road dwindled to nothing, a huge log cabin appeared in the rain. WELCOME TO LIBERTY blasted a sign above the door. The driver pulled up and shut off the engine. The sound of rain hitting the roof became suddenly apparent.

We stood, and stretched and fumbled about for our things. "Is it over?" I asked. "Are we really, actually there?"

Yannick glanced at me sympathetically. "I calculate," he said, "we've travelled five hundred kilometres. They weren't kidding when they called these the northern woods."

"They could at least have stopped for supper."

In the next instant, a brilliant flash dazzled our eyes. A crash of thunder followed immediately, with a presence that was almost physical. The rain's intensity increased until it looked like a solid sheet. The racket on the roof nearly drowned out conversation.

They opened the door at the front, but no one was getting off. That's when I heard the sound over the falling rain, an eerie, *group* sort of sound, rhythmic like ceremonial drums. Singing, I thought. Or chanting...

The two of us crammed in at the window to see. It was getting louder now, and the others were starting to notice. "You see anything?" I yelled.

Yannick shook his head. "A big cabin. Some little

ones. It must be coming from those. What kind of idiot would be out in this?"

As if in response, a stream of campers emerged from the woods, where they'd obviously gotten soaked. They all wore yellow T-shirts, and they all sort of skipped when they ran. They smiled, despite the rain streaming down their faces. Not one of them wore a raincoat.

"Wel-come to Li-ber-ty! Wel-come to Li-ber-ty! Wel-come to Li-ber-ty!..."

They joined hands, forming a complete circle around the bus. They began to dance sideways, skipping in perfect time to the rhythm of their chant.

"Wel-come to LI-BER-TY! Wel-come to LI-BER-TY!..."

Yannick turned to me, his eyes like saucers behind his glasses. "Surrealism City," he cried.

Julie and the driver were part of the frenzy. They went up and down the aisle, shaking people's hands, chanting along with the campers. Then the group outside started rocking the bus. Luggage began to fall from the overhead racks.

"WEL-COME TO LI-BER-TY! WEL-COME TO LI-BER-TY!..."

At the front of the bus Gunnarsson shouted something no one could hear; he seemed to have forgotten his microphone. It looked like he was asking us to step outside, but no one was taking him up on it. It was almost funny to see these guys in their twenties, scared to step off a bus.

Then a trio of yellow-shirts reached through the door and yanked the first one out. I watched in amazement as he was carried off on a river of hands, down the side of the bus. They went round the back, up the other side, and finally vanished into the largest cabin. Another passenger got sucked out after that, then another, and another. They each circled the bus before vanishing into the cabin, like litter swirling into a drain.

"This is nuts!" Yannick shouted, squeezing past me into the aisle; I guess he figured they'd leave him alone if he got off the bus on his own. "Welcome to Pandemonium! It's almost as if—*Jesus!*"

Up he went, carried off like a twig. I followed him seconds later.

The largest cabin turned out to be a sort of barn-shaped mess hall. Tables and chairs filled most of the space, arranged like a cafeteria. Loudspeakers hung above, suspended from fat wooden beams. And that was where order ended.

The place was a festival of confusion. Several of the yellow-shirted campers had gathered round a guy with a guitar and were singing at the top of their lungs. Another group nearby kept up the chant without a break. A third bunch were dancing some kind of chorus line. Above it all, people screamed out orders no one could possibly hear.

I spotted Yannick across the room, looking as bewildered as I felt. His was a comparatively familiar face, so I decided to head over there. I wondered how we'd wound up in different corners to begin with.

"Hello!" A smiling yellow-shirt stepped directly into my path. "My name's Ross. And you're—?"

"Corey. Corey Copeland."

"Hello, Corey. Welcome to Camp Liberty!" He consulted a clipboard. "Let's see, now, you'd be in Cabin Three—that's a good one, I had it last year. Hey, Mandy, let's show Corey to his cabin."

"Sure!" A skinny brunette bounced over, smiling despite her wet clothes. We stepped out again into the rain, where I claimed my one piece of luggage from the bus. Ross insisted on carrying it.

"So," said Mandy, skipping along beside me, "did you have a good trip in?"

"It was okay, I guess," I told her. "It took longer than I thought."

"Well, don't you worry," said Ross. "We'll get you into a good night's sleep."

"Right after supper, that is," said Mandy. "Well, here we are already."

We'd travelled maybe thirty feet. They could have simply pointed. "Thanks," I said anyway, wondering if they were a few bricks short.

"No problem," said Ross with a smile. Mandy opened the door for him and he set my duffel bag inside. "Please join us again in the mess hall as soon as you're settled in. You're going to love what we're having for supper!"

"We'll save you a place!" promised Mandy.

They smiled some more and left.

I entered to find the place empty, except for a half-dozen cots. All but one had been claimed with luggage. The last was at the back, where the roof slanted to four feet off the floor. It was darker there, but I could see where the ceiling had stained from water leaking in.

"Great," I muttered, but I dragged toward it anyway.

This vacation was going to be hell.

I lay on the cot. It wasn't really so damp, as long as I stayed on the left. I stretched, easing away cramps from the journey up. It was quiet. Only a muffled cheer floated through the wall from the direction of the mess hall. I stayed where I was, listening to rain on the roof, a lark chirping somewhere. And I realized where I was.

I was ten thousand light years away from the city, in a genuine wilderness. No crack houses. No street people. No gang wars, pimps, or junkies. And no mother, father or Marty to derail my every thought.

I took in the aroma of pine and breathed it out as a gentle sigh. Now, I thought, now I will relax. Now the pieces of my life will begin to fall into place, and I'll get that control I've wanted. The foreboding I'd felt on the bus gave way to a sense of peace.

It lasted maybe a minute.

Four

The door burst open with a suddenness that made me leap.

"Brother!" the entrant practically screamed, "you're going to miss your meal!"

I looked up to see a yellow-shirt standing in the doorway, a skinny, knob-kneed camper from hell. "Thanks," I muttered, rubbing my head where I'd struck the low ceiling. "I think I'm more tired than hungry, though."

"Oh, but Brother, it's more than just a meal! It's a rally for new arrivals. It's a great, big, welcoming..." he fumbled for words. "...group hug!"

I stared like you would at an idiot until someone I recognized came in behind him. "Oh, no!" Julie exclaimed. "You're going to miss your meal!"

One look at her, and I decided I was hungry after all. So I wound up letting them lead me to "hot dogs, chili and fellowship" at the mess hall. Julie waited while I loaded my plate, then stuffed in with me at the end of a long table.

I hadn't missed much, from the look of things. There was a lot of laughing, clapping and chanting going on, and here and there little foodfights. Some guy strummed a guitar, singing some folksy tune I'd never heard. Most of the new arrivals had already wolfed down their meals.

"Here," Julie said, sticking a name tag to my shirt. "Now everyone can get to know you, Brother Corey!" She took my hand and gave it a little squeeze. "Come on, eat your meal before it gets cold."

Someone began striking a glass with a fork. I looked up to see a low stage at the end of the room, where another table had been set. Gunnarsson was at its centre, with camp leaders to either side. As the room quietened, I noticed for the first time how we'd been arranged. Newcomers were scattered around the room, two or three to a table, sandwiched between veterans with yellow T-shirts.

Gunnarsson's voice boomed from the speakers above. "Welcome, campers! Welcome, new arrivals! Welcome, Brothers and Sisters of the Liberty Circle, to the start of another year!"

The yellow-shirts leapt to their feet and let out a mighty cheer. A few seconds later, they were seated again, as if it had never happened.

Gunnarsson looked about the room, a gleam of pride in his eye. When he spoke again, his voice was as intense as it had been on the bus.

"I don't think I need to remind you," he said, "that we are living in troubled times. Every day you hear of some new conflict in the world, of property being destroyed and people killed. Every day some country gets up and goes to war with its neighbour. Every day another nation gets hold of another weapon—maybe one they'll aim at you. We've reached the point where the drop of a feather could wipe us all away."

He pointed an accusatory finger and waved it about. "There is hunger in the world, increasing with the population. There are fewer and fewer jobs—some people have never known a steady one. So there is an increase in crime. There is alcoholism, broken families, riots touched off by people with nothing better to do! Let's face it, campers, society is going to hell in a teapot!"

That touched off a few nervous laughs. "Are we having fun yet?" asked one of the new arrivals.

Gunnarsson held up a hand. "All right—I'm not going to give you a lecture. What I want to say is simply this: all of the world's troubles can be traced to one simple fact: we don't all think alike.

"Can you imagine every nation adopting true democracy? It would be *Utopia*. There'd be hardly a social problem left to deal with. Oh, sure, we'd still have natural problems—like disease, or earthquakes—but even those would be closer to a solution. Without the expense of defence budgets, research and social programs could increase a thousand-fold. Unemployment would vanish. Even natural disasters could be controlled." His voice fell until it was barely audible.

"But we just don't all think alike, do we? No. And we never shall."

He came around the long table and strode toward the edge of the stage. "You will find, at Camp Liberty, an unusual method of learning. We believe in order to understand why people act as they do, it is necessary to get inside their heads—to actually feel what *they* feel. Only then can we understand the human condition, and work at bettering it.

"If you could understand just one fringe group, one bad element of society, you would be closer to understanding them all. So you will learn—for a time—to actually become members of one of these fringes. This summer, you are going to be Nazis."

We newcomers burst out laughing. Gunnarsson didn't even crack a smile.

"We'll only be pretending, of course. But I have to warn you, campers, this is one intensive experiment. If past seasons are any indication, *some of you may actually begin to believe you are Nazis.*"

"But Mr. Gunnarsson," chirped one of the yellow-shirts, "how will changing us into Nazis make the world a better place?"

"You won't leave here as such, of course," Gunnarsson replied. "If some of you adopt their ideologies for a time, so much the better. You will then understand how they feel. But we won't let you remain fanatics. You'll go through a debriefing period later. And you will leave here better equipped to fight bigotry and hatred, to deal with differences between peoples." He gazed across his audience. "Are there any other questions?"

There were, a flurry of them:

"How long will this experiment take?"

"We should be finished in two or three days."

"Is this part of the fun?"

"At first you'll find it quite gruelling. But ultimately, you'll enjoy it like nothing you've ever experienced."

"What happens if I get 'programmed', then called home in an emergency?"

Gunnarsson waved a hand. "That will be dealt with

tomorrow. We'll have a meeting then, recapping the first day's progress."

At the table next to me, a dark-haired boy raised his hand. He was one of the new arrivals and one of the few my age. "What happens," he demanded, "if we don't get 'programmed' at all? I don't think anyone could 'program' me."

Gunnarsson smiled weakly. "We'll see, Tony," he said.

With the questions exhausted, Gunnarsson returned to his place at the table. "A few last very important words," he said grimly. "This is the experiment that isn't; once we start, you must believe that it's real. Don't talk about it, even in your leisure time, as though it were only a game. That is the most important rule, and I can hardly stress it too much. If the experiment is to succeed, you must try to believe that you are really Nazis.

"And remember, it'll get intense. Don't try to fight it, though—just go with your feelings. Remember, we'll be cancelling out any negative thoughts you might pick up, later on.

"We will now begin."

The room went completely black—and stayed like that for over a minute. A stunned silence slowly gave way to a curious buzz. I was maybe more curious than most; I'd known Gunnarsson for ages and had never seen him like this.

The lights came back on and the mess hall erupted with laughter. Gunnarsson was exactly where he'd been before—except now in full Nazi uniform. He even had the swastika armband.

"Silence!" he roared, and his anger seemed so genuine

that we all shut up immediately. Some of the yellow-shirts went around passing out Nazi armbands.

"Put them on," Gunnarsson ordered.

We did, though of course we newcomers treated it like a joke.

"Heil Hitler." He gave the Nazi salute.

"Heil Hitler," we responded, completely out of unison and snickering our heads off. Some guys used the wrong arm.

"STOP!" It was a scream, not a shout. The echo of it buzzed through the silence long after, passing through the rafters. "You think this is a game? Heil Hitler! Together—*Heil Hitler!*"

"Heil Hitler." More synchronized now. Nervous.

"There is a film," he said, his voice clipped. "You will watch it, and you will learn about—" he paused dramatically "—*the way things are.*"

As he spoke, the yellow-shirts rushed to get things ready. Two TV monitors were wheeled into place, one on either side of the stage. The loudspeakers crackled with static, and the lights went out again.

It started with a growl, a sound that chilled me to the core, though I couldn't guess what it was. Then the monitors flickered to life.

It was like a video collage of the worst of everything that had ever happened. We saw fragments of news reports and documentaries, mixed together in a manner that was downright eerie. Images overlapped and blended together, until you couldn't be sure of what you were seeing.

We looked at one bloody mess after another—the

human debris of wars and terrorism, people dead or dying. We saw missiles, aimed at us from grain silos, submarines and airplanes. We saw what nuclear bombs had done to others, and what they could do to us. We saw enough to make us sick—the screens were like windows to hell.

I looked away for a moment, but couldn't block out the sounds. Screams and cries played against a background of noises you couldn't identify. It was like Death, or Satan himself, screaming out your name. An icy coldness entered my spine and spread throughout my body. I glanced at a screen again and saw a crimson skull grinning back at me just for an instant.

It ended abruptly, as if a switch had been thrown. In the resulting darkness, Gunnarsson spoke:

"That is the way things are. Tomorrow, you will learn who made them that way—and why."

The lights came on again. I'd hardly touched my meal, but the sight of food now made me nauseous. One of the girls was crying.

"Heil Hitler!" Gunnarsson threw out his arm.

"Heil Hitler!" we responded, welcoming the diversion. "Heil Hitler! Heil Hitler! Heil Hitler!"

The chant soon became almost as overpowering as the video itself. When they threw open the mess hall doors, we exploded into the night like sparks. No one spoke at all until we were safely back in our cabins.

"That was strange," Tony remarked when we got to Cabin Three. Counting him and myself, there were five of us new arrivals. Yannick wasn't among us, but neither were Keith or his skinhead friend. The sixth resident of the cabin was one of the yellow-shirts.

"Just too unbelievably strange," Tony reiterated, when no one else responded. He reached into his duffel bag and pulled out a ghetto-blaster. He frowned, and looked about. "My stupid batteries are missing! I could swear I put them in. Where's a plug-in?"

"There are none." The yellow-shirt smiled benignly. "We have everything we need already—beds for a good night's sleep. I am Brother Allan. Welcome, friends, to the freedom of Camp Liberty! Heil Hitler!"

"Yeah, good," snapped Tony. "Who's got a flashlight?"

"They told us not to bring any," I said. "They were supposed to be supplying them."

"And we will," said Brother Allan. "When they are needed."

"Aw, hell," said Tony. He gazed up at the single light. "Well, maybe we could plug into that. If we could get one of those—what the hell?"

The bulb had started to dim, like in a theatre before the show. Brother Allan smiled sweetly.

"Lights-out," he said, just as we were plunged into night.

You can pretty much guess our reaction to that. It was weird, though: within minutes, everybody got real quiet.

I mean, we spoke to each other at first, ignoring Allan's pleas to "get a good night's rest". But soon, disembodied voices from other cots got slow and heavy-sounding. One by one, the others dropped from conversation. In the end, it was Tony and me.

"I'm from a lousy neighbourhood, too," he was

saying, his voice reduced to a mumble. "But I really came...to get away from my dad..."

"My family's no great shakes, either," I admitted. "Hey, Tony, have you ever been here before? Tony?"

No reply.

I sat up. Now this was really weird. "Mark?" I said. "Dave? Brother Allan?"

Silence. Even the rain had stopped.

I lay back in bed with a sigh. These guys had faded out like that bulb...and I couldn't get to sleep! It was because of the video, I knew. Here I was, a zillion miles from nowhere in a cabin in the pines, and all I could think of was the missiles, the way they were aimed at me right now. I could almost hear the screams of those who had died, the cries of those in grief. The video played itself out in my brain, then rewound and played again. It was in the middle of the tenth showing before I finally started to drift.

Then, one second away from sleep, my eyes snapped open. What was that?

I rolled over in my cot and faced the wall at the back of the cabin. There, just above the threshold of hearing: a vague, tiny sound, too slight to recognize. Whispers, maybe. Sighs. A noise like a silent scream. It came from outside and was almost indistinguishable from the sound of rustling leaves. But maybe that's all it was.

Exhaustion eventually caught up with me, and I slept at last. I dreamed of leaves, rustling in the dark, in a place where only evergreens grew.

Five

I woke before the others, with that eerie sensation you get after a nightmare. The cabin was grey with morning twilight. I remembered the noise I'd heard and lay still in my bed to listen. The only sounds now were the breathing of my companions and the trill of a loon on the lake.

I should take out my paints, I thought, *or go down to the water and sketch*. But another deep breath of pine, and I drifted away again.

When I woke the second time, the woods were a hum of activity—and I do mean hum. There was a choir outside doing exactly that.

"No-o-o-o-o!" Mark, the chubby guy in our group, buried his face in his pillow. "Make them go away."

But the door banged open, and the choir stuck in its smiling heads. A dozen yellow-shirted campers burst into happy song:

"Good morning! Good morning!
It's time you were awake!
It's five o'clock, the rain has stopped,
Get up, for goodness sake!"

"Jesus." I sat up, rubbing my eyes. "It's like camping with 'Up With People'."

"Did they say *five o'clock*?" asked Tony incredulously.

"We are the Aryan youth,
We stand so brave and proud,
We want to say, we're back to stay,
We want to shout it LOUD!
Heil Hitler! Heil Hitler! Heil Hitler!"

Brother Allan, already dressed, hopped sprightly from his cot. "Come, join us, fellow campers. Let's form an Aryan mambo line!"

"Form it yourself," snapped Tony, lying back in bed.

But one at a time, we each got yanked out onto the soaking grass. They actually made us form this mambo line, at five o'clock in the morning, with the sun just creaking over the horizon. Those who objected—like me—were cooed and fussed over by the women.

"Come on, Mark, don't be left out!"

"We *like* you, Corey!"

"Everyone else is doing it—be a good sport!"

"That's it, you've got it now! Three cheers for Mark and Corey!"

We mamboed through the camp from cabin to cabin, waking everyone the same stupid way. Finally, we hit the mess hall for breakfast. *That* was a disappointment: cold cereal with watered-down milk. Troubles with the grill, they told us. Meantime, the yellow-shirts kept prancing around the hall, pestering and chanting continuously. Didn't they ever stop to eat?

At our table, Allan rose to address us. "We've got a big day ahead of us," he shouted above the din. "Mr. Gunnarsson will be leading a rally right after breakfast, then we'll be going on a hike with the gals from Cabin Nine. After that, we've got some real heavy-duty fun lined up.

"But remember," he cautioned, "don't forget the experiment. For the next two or three days, you are Nazis." He stood, slapped his heels together, and struck out an arm in salute. "Heil Hitler!"

We laughed. It was too early for that crap.

Allan's face clouded, but before he could say anything, Julie swooped in with her charges from Cabin Nine.

"Hi! How's everyone doing? Are you ready for some FUN? Good! Let's all hop on over to the Bowl!"

"Good idea!" said Allan. "In fact, let's hop like rabbits!" He dropped to a squat and stuck up his fingers to look like ears. "Hop! Hop! Hop! Come on, guys, work with me on this! Hop! Hop! Hop!"

Reluctantly, one by one by one, the others fell in behind him. I could not believe my eyes. Making fools of themselves seemed less embarrassing to them than being ridiculed for not joining in.

"C'mon, Corey, join us! Everyone else is doing it!"

"The Bowl" was a grassy valley nearby, where trees had been felled to serve as benches. In the centre, a giant boulder embedded in the earth served as a speaker's stage. Everyone in the camp was there, about fifty or so in all. More than half wore yellow T-shirts. I wondered when we new arrivals would be getting ours.

"Good morning, campers!" Gunnarsson had mounted

the boulder, microphone in hand. His voice blasted from speakers in the trees surrounding us. The yellow-shirts went briefly nuts, just like they had last night. You'd have thought Christ himself had showed.

Gunnarsson merely smiled and made a half-hearted gesture for silence. He was wearing his Nazi uniform. "Campers!" he exclaimed when the racket had died away. "Have I got a story to tell. It's going to knock you off your feet. It's going to frighten you. It's going to change the way you look at the world. And it's a story that must be told.

"The world is the way it is by *plan*, not by accident. Everything that happens does so because of a massive conspiracy—a gigantic plot by a certain group of people who want the planet under their control. Wars, famine, crime, the breakdown in social structure, all of these occur as results of this conspiracy.

"All men are not created equal, and scientific proof exists of that. Some races are more highly evolved than others. We Aryans—white folks of non-Jewish descent— we are the master race. All others fall below. God's plan was to have the Aryans rule over all.

"The Zionists, the Jews, are the leaders of the conspiracy. They want to enslave the other races and destroy the one above them—us. In this way, they hope to gain control of the world. The biggest weapon they have at their disposal is communism—which has many more faces than you think.

"But let's take it from the top, and go through each of these points in detail..."

He went on like that for an hour, until it no longer

sounded like a game. I don't mean that I believed him or anything—just that it would be easy to if you'd never been to school and learned the truth. But then, according to Gunnarsson, even the history books were lying.

"You've been cheated," he snarled. "You've been lied to. Our government is full of conspirators who suppress us at every turn. Income tax, for example—another contrivance to hold us down. And the Holocaust of World War Two? A holo-hoax. Six million dead Jews, all right—you'll find them in Toronto...Vancouver...New York."

He was starting to sound like he believed his own speech.

We all listened carefully; he had a way of holding your attention, even when you knew he was only acting. When he finished, and did the salute, we returned it enthusiastically. It was just a game, after all.

We went on the promised hike, cabins Three and Nine together. That meant jogging down rain-moistened trails where mosquitoes whined through the undergrowth. My breathing got faster and harder, but not as fast or hard as the counsellors. Both Allan and Julie looked exhausted. It was like they never slept.

The trail ended at a clearing by a gate in the chain link fence—a fence that apparently surrounded the entire camp. I noticed for the first time the barbed wire that topped it off. What was *that* for? I wondered. It must have cost a mint.

"That's to keep out the bears," Allan said, catching my gaze. He regarded me a moment with a bright, sharp gaze. Then he clapped his hands together and looked about the group. "All right. Everyone sit themselves down in a circle, and we'll pass around the old water jug. And while we're at it, let's each tell everyone our name and a little bit about ourselves."

One of those deals. So we all sat there telling our little tales, slapping at mosquitoes the size of bats. Most of the campers were in college, or between jobs, or otherwise uncertain of the future. Even Julie had been like that once: "I thought I had goals," she said, "until I came here. Then I realized how dull it all was—go to college, get a plain old job, lead an average life. Well, Camp Liberty changed all that. Now I have a real chance at changing the world."

Allan nodded. "I was the same way. I thought I wanted to work in a bank, become a manager. Then I met Peter Gunnarsson, who showed me there was more to life than money. Now I'm in college, learning to be a teacher—the Liberty Circle way."

I was about to ask what the Liberty Circle was when we were interrupted by a commotion. Someone was approaching from camp—fast. Whoever it was crashed right through the brush, ignoring the zigzagging trail. Then we heard a wail like a yowling cat and voices muffled by the forest.

Allan stood, his face the colour of paper. He looked like he expected a bear to come racing out on the wrong side of the fence. But a yellow-shirted woman appeared instead and ran straight across to the gate.

"No-o-o-o!" she cried, struggling with a padlock. "It's got to open!"

Now *I* expected a bear, but the only thing that followed was more yellow-shirted campers.

"Angie, wait!"

"Don't run from us, Angie, please—we're your friends!"

"Angie, you don't understand!"

They swooped on her, five in all, as she started to climb the gate. Her cries turned to screams, and there was no doubting the reality of the tears streaming down her face. It took all of them holding her firmly to lead her back up the trail. One, a big guy with a beard, smiled back at Allan.

"It's okay, Brother. We'll take care of her."

"Take her to Palmer," Allan replied. "She needs reinforcement." In a low voice, he added, "I *told* you..."

The beard nodded, and the yellow-shirts vanished up the trail with their human cargo. We could still hear her cries, though—and then suddenly they were forming words: "Run! Get away! They want to change your minds! They want—"

Her voice was cut off abruptly. In a few seconds, the forest was as silent as before.

"What the hell was that all about?" Tony demanded. We looked to Allan for an explanation.

He seemed embarrassed and glanced at Julie nervously. "Angie is... Well, she's—"

"Sick," Julie put in. "Very sick, actually."

"Is it...drugs?" asked a girl from Cabin Nine.

Julie nodded. "I'm afraid so, Diane. We are...working with Angie, trying to get her back into the mainstream of life. She's actually been doing quite well. It's just that now and then she has these..."

"Setbacks," Allan supplied.

With that explained, we rose to return to camp. We started out silently, subdued by what we'd seen, until Allan and Julie insisted we sing. That's not easy when you're jogging, but everyone seemed to warm into it after a while. Everyone but me, that is.

There'd been something wrong with that explanation, I thought, something fake. They'd seemed stumped for a moment, then the words had tumbled out. And Allan's comment: *Take her to Palmer. She needs reinforcement.* Who the hell was Palmer? And what was "reinforcement"?

Julie caught me looking at her and gave me a questioning smile. I looked away immediately, feeling a blush spread across my face; she was movie star gorgeous. But there was something else, too, something in her eyes. Something that said, I know that you know.

I shook my head. I was getting paranoid, I decided. I didn't know anything.

I couldn't quite keep my mind from wandering, though, and my eyes were to meet hers twice more before we got back to camp.

Six

"G o, Satan, go! Go, Satan, go!" We "angels" screamed our heads off as the "devil"—in the chubby form of Mark—raced once more around the course. He made it on time for once and hurled the ball at the net. He missed—again.

"Next demon!" shouted Allan, drowning out our groans. There was only one other left, the slight girl named Diane. "Come on, Sister, you can do it. Show us how to get to Heaven."

Diane gave it all she had, for the fourth time in a row, but couldn't even make the course. She wound up in the mud, wiping away a tear.

"I feel so awkward," she said. "I feel like a goose."

Julie helped her to her feet. "There's nothing wrong with geese. In fact, let's all be geese!" And she dropped to a squat, stuck her elbows out like wings, and proceeded to hobble along like a bird. "Gobble, gobble. Gobble, gobble, gobble."

"Come on, campers, let's follow Julie's lead!" Allan dropped into place behind her, the "Satan" game apparently abandoned. "Gobble! Gobble, gobble!"

Automatically, the others joined in; they'd learned

how useless it was to object. I stayed where I was, half-hidden beneath a pine. We'd been doing crap like this all day. It was getting more than a little strange.

Suddenly, a giddy little feeling of excitement entered my chest. The "geese" were waddling off without me—they hadn't noticed me missing! I sat absolutely still, praying Allan or Julie wouldn't glance back. If they caught me hiding like this, I'd never get any peace.

"Un-be-liev-a-ble."

I spun to see Yannick standing behind me, in the shadow of the lowest bows. He wasn't even with our group. His eyes went wide behind his glasses as he watched the "geese" go by. He gave me a baffled look.

"They let you take a break?"

I shook my head. "I just sort of forgot to follow them."

"Yeah. Yeah, same here." He came and sat beside me, glancing cautiously about. "They practically follow you into the can," he said. "And talk about your non-stop 'fun'. They don't let up for an instant. Plus, one moment we're organized, then the next, it's total chaos. Either way, there's always noise."

I grunted. "There has to be. They seem to get upset with us if there isn't."

"So far today I've mamboed through breakfast, run a three-legged race with a mannequin, imitated barnyard animals and attended a tea party with invisible furniture."

"I can top that," I told him, because I could. But before I got a chance to say how, a voice cut through the woods behind us.

"Brother Yannick! I've been looking all over for you." A yellow-shirt came charging out toward us. "You're going to miss your lunch!"

"My caretaker," Yannick muttered. But we got up and followed the guy to the mess hall; lunch was an hour late as it was. My group was there already, and Allan was waiting for me.

"Brother Corey—there you are! We were getting worried!" As if I'd been dragged off by a bear or something. He and another yellow-shirt led me firmly to the table. After that, I was hardly allowed to feed myself; practically everything was done for me. I knew it, I thought, I knew it. They'd be on me now like fleas on a dog.

After a fifteen minute meal of lukewarm, diluted soup, the entire camp was herded down to the beach for canoe lessons. There, a sombre guy named Jordan ran us quickly through the basics. I do mean quickly, too—we were in the water inside of ten minutes. Each cabin got its own canoe.

"Pull! Pull! Pull!" Allan sat at the back of the boat, shouting his head off. Naturally, he wasn't rowing.

"Pull! Pull! Pull!" Cabin Six's canoe edged up beside ours. Its leader grinned at Allan. Allan looked at us.

"We aren't going to let those guys pass us, are we?"

"Yes!" gasped Mark behind me. "We are!"

But behind him, Tony laughed a bit wildly, and I heard the splash of an oar cutting deeper into the water. Despite a dizziness from lousy food and lack of sleep, I had to smile. We were getting better, and Cabin Six was falling behind.

"Deeper, Mark, deeper! Not so high on return, Brent!

That's it! Pull! Pull! Pull! Say it with me!" Our chant echoed across the water, falling into sync with identical chants from other canoes. Soon we were all shouting the same thing, making simultaneous strokes, in a dozen canoes stretching across the lake.

It went on like that—non-stop—for at least another two hours.

The chanting became the sound of a machine, blasting into my brain. I was an unthinking part, a piston or something, driven only by noise. Sweat burned into my eyes, until it became easier to keep them closed. My arms went numb and I lost track of where they were. It didn't matter. The chant kept them perfectly timed.

"Pull! Pull! Pull! Pull! Pull! Pull! Pull!"

I could sense the effort of Mark behind me, struggling to keep up speed. I could almost picture the fat changing to sweat, then burning off into the atmosphere. I could sure as hell smell it.

I began to feel sick.

Then I went beyond sick, into a state of mind where Camp Liberty was all that existed: its farthest flung edges were those of the universe.

"Pull! Pull! Pull! Okay, stop. Whoa! Corey!"

Canoe Three blasted onto the beach, and I fell backwards into Mark's lap.

We pulled the canoe onto the sand, an eternity after we'd left. I didn't fall over, throw up or faint dead away, though it felt like I'd do all three. I just stood by the water's edge, worried I'd drop if I moved at all. I was vaguely aware of others who already had.

There was movement in one direction, like cattle

heading for the corral. I stayed right where I was until someone touched my arm.

"Corey? It's me, Dave. You'd better come to the Bowl. There's a fellow here from Texas who's going to be giving a speech. They want us there to hear it."

It took me a moment to recognize my cabinmate. I grabbed at his arm. "Tony was right," I gasped. "This place is really strange. Something's definitely wrong."

Dave looked at me closely. "What are you talking about?"

I shook my head. I didn't know. I didn't know anything.

"Look," he said, taking my ar,. "it's weird, I know. I'm feeling it too. But Peter Gunnarsson knows what he's doing. I'm sure of it. Let's just go with the flow for now." He led me to the Bowl as he spoke.

I wound up between Allan and another yellow-shirt. On the boulder/stage in front of me, a man with a hamburger-patty face was making another point.

"You got to play the game," he was saying. "Our enemies have been playing the game, but here in the free world we keep forgetting to. We figure now that the Soviet menace is gone, it's okay to drop our guard. But that is exactly what the Jewish-commie conspirators would lead us to believe!

"The menace ain't gone, it just moved to the Third World. All those tinpot dictators running those banana republics—who do you think's pulling their strings? And while they stockpile nuclear weapons, the peaceniks here would have us take apart NATO. Well, they're all part of the conspiracy, too! And our Zionist-occupied government is just liable to go along.

"The Jews ain't even really people, you know. Jews and niggers were God's experiments. He didn't create the perfect human being till the final day of Creation. And that human, my friends, was an Aryan. Proof exists of that. Non-Aryans ain't human at all. Like animals, they got no souls.

"They're mud-people."

My head was whirling from too many hours of chanting, singing and exercise, too few hours of sleep. I was hungry, too—couldn't they at least feed us right? I'd been weak enough from lack of food before I'd even come there. I couldn't tell any more if what I was hearing made sense. I couldn't even tell if it was part of the game; the line between reality and make believe was getting as blurry as my vision.

"I don't feel too well," I mumbled, but Allan brushed me off.

"Shhhh! Pay attention, Corey. This part is very important."

The speaker sat on the edge of the boulder. I noticed for the first time the battle fatigues and the cap that said "KKK". "The commies got the right idea," he said. "They knew by moving their power base to these two-bit countries, we'd let our guard down. And that's why we have to watch more than ever before. The time has never been better for them to strike!"

I willed him to finish, to stop talking, so we could return to our cabins and get some sleep. Supper, which was overdue already, no longer seemed to matter. I was too ill and exhausted to eat. But as the sun dipped below the horizon, someone set up a slide projector.

We sat through scene after scene of life in the Third World, and it wasn't what you'd see on a travel brochure. We saw missiles, tanks and spy satellites. We saw line-ups for food. We saw a classroom, in whatever they call a high school. There was writing on the blackboard, in English.

"Why," cried Beef-face triumphantly, "do you suppose these young people are learning English? Just think about that for a while." He clicked the projector once more and the screen went blank.

There was movement again, this time toward the mess hall. I hadn't even heard the command. I walked along unsteadily for a moment, then stopped. Something was wrong. The world was spinning on its axis as always, but I could actually see it.

I don't even remember hitting the ground.

Seven

For days, and nights, and days again, we danced and sang and chanted. Time stretched and compressed, until finally it meant nothing. We played games, aimed at "enlightening" us, that only made me confused. In one, the meanings of words would change and everyone would act as if it had always been that way. After a while, I would wonder if it hadn't. After a while, I would wonder if I was going insane.

I dreamed a lot when I slept, wild dreams of wild things. When I woke, reality would often be stranger. Before long, the two became difficult to tell apart. And sometimes, I think, I dreamed when I was awake.

There came the night I was shaken from sleep by Allan screaming into my ear:

"Get up, Brother Corey! The communists are attacking!"

We went out, dressed completely in black fatigues and armed with red-lensed flashlights. Other shapes moved nearby, campers from other cabins. I could hear that sound from the woods again: the rustling of leaves that weren't. The stench of forest-fire smoke added an eerie heaviness to the air.

There was a brilliant green flash from the woods and a sound like an Indian war cry. "They're in there!" someone shouted. "Go after them, *now!*"

I dimly remember lurching ahead, dodging dewy branches, wondering why I was doing this at three in the morning. Cones of red and green swung wildly through the trees, and there were muffled shouts from the dark. Then Tony and I cornered a "commie". He squatted amongst the ferns, his back turned, ignoring us entirely.

My annoyance shot to the surface. Here we were, being devoured by mosquitoes, and this jerk was just prolonging it. I grabbed him by the shoulder.

"Come on, fool," I snapped. "Let's get back to camp so we can all go back to—"

Our captive spun around, snarling like a dog. He was a werewolf.

A clawed hand struck out and smacked me in the face. Next thing you know I was down in the weeds, and he was crashing off into the woods. Tony started after him, but it was no use; he had too much of a head start. When the crimson light worked its way back to me, I was still sitting there, unidentifiable crawling objects exploring my shirt.

"You should have caught him," Tony said.

"He was a werewolf," I mused, holding a hand to my throbbing face. "A bloody werewolf, with fangs yet."

"It was a trick, meant to startle you."

"No kidding."

"You should have caught him."

"Hey!" I scrambled to my feet, rage building in my chest. "What the hell's wrong with you? It's just a game.

A stupid game, like all the other stupid games we've been playing!"

Tony faced me eye to eye, his face lit eerily by the flashlight. "What makes you so sure that this is all a game?" He stared just long enough to let me know he was serious, then he turned and started back to camp.

I followed slowly, exhaustion catching up. Was I going nuts, I wondered? Or could it be everyone else? The part of my brain that could answer that was completely out of commission. I had to get away. I had to leave this camp, or I'd never know for sure.

I decided I'd better sleep first—I could hardly even walk. When I'd rested, and was thinking clearly, *then* I would make my break. But guards were posted everywhere, making sure no one returned to their cabins. Head for the Bowl, they told us. They're going to pass out books.

"Come on, Brother Corey, we'd love to have you there."

"Don't let us down!"

"This is really, really important. You won't want to miss this."

For what seemed like the millionth time, I was led by the hand to the Bowl. It was this hand-holding business, I decided, that more than anything was driving me nuts. I longed to have people stop touching me.

We got the books. They were real books, hard-cover, not something made at camp. And they were all about the conspiracy. I shook my head, trying to sort it out. Maybe the game was based on the books, rather than the other way around.

"What do you think?" Julie was there, looking over my shoulder. Julie was always there.

"I don't understand it," I said. "These say the conspiracy is real."

"Yes," she replied, "they do."

"But that's impossible."

"Is it?" She touched my arm. "Look, Corey, just trust us, okay? It'll all be explained at the end. Like Mr. Gunnarsson said, don't worry how it'll affect you." She ran her fingers through my hair. "Just stay with it," she cooed. "For me?"

So I stayed with it once more, for Julie. I listened to endless speeches and watched slides and films and videos, as the sky slowly lightened again. All the while, a sensation grew in the back of my mind, something deeper than my deepest fears. I felt there was a horrible truth lurking around the corner, something waiting to be known that I would rather have stayed a mystery.

Sunrise came, softly diffused by smoke. It was right about then that the new arrivals began disappearing, one at a time. They'd return with clouded eyes, unwilling to speak of where they'd been. They would send the next person. Despite the best efforts of the yellow-shirts, a rumour managed to work its way round the Bowl: it was a test of some kind, designed to find out how much we'd learned. It was not an easy test.

Yannick came back when the sun was just over the horizon. He spotted me from across the Bowl and walked directly over. "It's your turn," he said. His face was as pale as the new morning sky.

"What's it about?" I asked, my voice uneven.

He shook his head and gazed into the distance. "It's about...everything." He turned back to me and his eyes were lit, as if he'd spotted a city of gold perched up on the clouds. "I'm not supposed to say. Just go, down that path."

I went where he said, eventually reaching a clearing at the top of a hill. There was a picnic table here, at which sat Peter Gunnarsson. He was smoking a cigarette. Beside him was a little cage.

"Hello, Corey. How are you this morning?"

"Okay, I guess. Tired."

"Uh-huh. Corey, do you know what this is, in the cage?"

"A squirrel?"

"That's right. Cute, isn't it? It's a male, I believe, probably a daddy with a wife and kids to feed. You're something of an artist, aren't you? I'll bet this would be a challenge to paint. Just look at the colours."

I looked, and the squirrel looked back with bright, animal eyes. Its fur was every colour of the country—charcoal, clay, wood, blended impossibly. It was nature itself, I thought. A symbol of everything the city wasn't.

"I want you," said Gunnarsson, "to kill it."

I blinked. "What?"

"I want you to kill it, Corey, and I don't mean mercifully. Let me tell you how."

He did, and I felt sick. "I can't do that."

"Sure you can. To be a Nazi, you must be willing to do anything. You cannot have pity. You must, at times, be absolutely without feeling. Remember everything you've learned. Don't worry. It's only a dumb animal."

I thought of everything they'd taught me, everything that had happened since my arrival—how many days ago? I thought of all the others who had taken this test already.

"You aren't a coward, are you, Corey?"

"No."

I reached for the cage.

I did what he told me. I don't want to tell about that. I don't even want to think about it.

When it was over, something snapped inside me, something precious like fine glass. I felt a surge of nausea, and I spun away to the grass to be ill. I looked up to see him standing there, calmly smoking. For a moment, I wanted to kill him. I wanted to scream, "You see what you've made me do? You think I'm weak because I couldn't do it without emotion. But it's because I'm stronger than the others that I feel something. You can't change me!" But I didn't say anything.

He pulled the cigarette from his mouth. "I have asked over twenty others to do what you just did," he said. "Each had the precise same task to perform. You are the first to actually do it."

I scrambled to my feet and ran, blindly, away from him and his camp. It seemed I'd been running forever when I reached the perimeter fence. There was another clearing here, and a gate. This was where we'd gone hiking before.

I looked at the padlocked gate. It was topped off with barbed wire, but it would still be possible to climb. Beyond that was a forest infested with bears. That wouldn't stop me either.

But then a sort of darkness lifted from my brain, and I suddenly saw everything clearly. All the chanting, all the songs, all the crazy, mixed-up games—I saw now where all of it led. With a moan, I fell to the ground and put my hands over my head. The secret that had been growling in the wings leapt out at me now with teeth. All I could do was let it.

Gunnarsson caught up a few seconds later, not even breathing hard from the run. He sat quietly down beside me, and I'm sure he was waiting for the question I asked—the one I didn't really want an answer to: "It's real, isn't it? The conspiracy is real."

Gunnarsson nodded. "Yes. It is real."

I covered my head again, and I guess I started to cry. He put a hand on my shoulder.

"It was easier for you," he said, "to believe the world was the way you thought. It was easier to live each day as though nothing was wrong, as though everyone on earth was equal and there were no lower races plotting to take away your freedom. You could make your plans and dream your dreams, all in blissful ignorance. But it wouldn't last, Corey. Sooner or later the conspirators would make their move, and your world would be destroyed. It is better for you to know. This way, you can do something about it."

I shook my head, still not wanting to believe. "But why did you call it a game?"

"Would you have listened to me if I hadn't?"

No, I thought. I would not have.

He stood up. "Come on, Corey. It's time to begin your new life, as a defender of the Aryan race and Freedom."

I know better now. It took me a long time to get things straight, to sort my way through those lies. But there, in those woods with the smoke flowing through them, after all those lousy meals and non-stop activities, after days with little sleep, it all seemed to make sense. It was as though Camp Liberty had taken me apart, then used the pieces to build something else—something I never thought I'd be.

After a few minutes, I got up and let Peter Gunnarsson lead me to my new life.

Eight

A concert of buses, boom boxes and sirens surged in through an open window at the end of the corridor. It blended with noises from other suites: babies crying, someone arguing, a TV up turned too loud. No sound at all came from inside our apartment door. I stood just outside it with a couple of Brothers, and I trembled.

"Remember," whispered Brother Allan, "you must fight for control of your thoughts at all times. Think of nothing but the Liberty Circle. Your family may knock you off-track, make you think of yourself. That's when you must recite the chant, the one to ward off unapproved thought. You must never think of yourself, only of the Circle."

I nodded. "I won't forget, Brother Allan."

"I wish you could come with us to Liberty Hall—but that will happen soon enough. In the meantime, don't forget you can call, any time, for anything. If you feel yourself slipping, run away. Come to us for reinforcement. Chant. And, Brother Corey—don't miss a fellowship meeting for anything."

"I won't."

"Another thing: distance your beliefs from the Circle.

If they know you're part of our group, they'll try to get you out. That's what they did with Brother Mort here when he dropped out of college to join us. He was kidnapped, Corey, and fed conspiracy lies until he nearly cracked. Fortunately, he escaped and came back to us in time."

"They call it 'deprogramming'," Mort added. It was the first time I'd heard him speak. "It's bad."

"It's the worst thing that can happen to you," Allan said, "as we've warned you many times." He glanced about, then gave me a quick salute. "Heil Hitler, Brother Corey. Don't forget a thing you've learned."

I entered our apartment quietly, not wishing to announce my return just yet. By design, we were home a day early, so my arrival would be unexpected. That was part of the plan. I had no idea why. But I'd learned not to question the plans of our "Leader"—the one who gave Gunnarsson his orders, the one who could never reveal his name or his face. The one they didn't even tell us about until four days before we left camp.

I crept through the place like a ghost, but I could have spared myself the trouble: no one was home. At least, that's what I thought until I entered my room.

"*Cripes!*" Marty flipped upright in my bed, knocking over the bedside lamp. "Man, Corey, don't you ever knock?"

As if it wasn't my own room. I just stood there staring at the two of them and wondering what the old Corey would have done. Valerie stared back evenly, her eyes gleaming as if in triumph.

"Get out of my bed," I said flatly.

"Corey, man, I'm real sorry about this. We didn't

think you were back till tomorrow. The sofa bed's kind of awkward, and—"

"Get out of my room."

"All right." He held up a hand. "We're going."

Valerie made a circling motion with her finger. "Turn around, Goldilocks."

I did, long enough to sling my duffel bag into the closet.

The second they were gone, I ripped all the blankets and sheets off the bed and threw them into the hall. That included Marty's pillow, which struck his head with satisfying force. I returned to my room, locked the door and lay back across the mattress.

I stared at the ceiling. It seemed to be turning slightly, as if it weren't quite in sync with me. I squeezed my eyes tight. Just a hint of the nausea that had plagued me the last week of camp. It would feel good, so good, to take a long, cold shower and sleep off the rest of the afternoon. But I wouldn't.

I got up and went to work. First, the bookshelves by the window. Not much I could do here—it was hard to tell who was Aryan and who wasn't. No, wait, this one. A story about blacks, written by one, even. And this one here... I tossed them onto my bed. They would do well at the book burning the following week.

Next I turned to my ghetto blaster and the few cassettes I owned. I was in the middle of weeding those out when Marty's voice cut through the door.

"Cor—pick up the phone. It's Lisa."

Lisa? I stepped into the hall, annoyed. Lisa wouldn't know I was back. But the phone dangled by its cord in the hall, and I picked it up just to be sure. It was Lisa, all right.

"*Why the hell didn't you write me?*"

"I was...busy. They kept us busy right from the time we got there."

"I'm sure they did," she replied dryly. "I thought I'd get back from Montreal to find a half-dozen letters from you."

"How did you know I was home?"

"I didn't. I took a chance. Corey, I need you here—like, now. And dress up. Mom's thrown this huge party to announce her running for council. There's going to be a lot of bigwigs here, and she went and invited their kids. I don't even know them all. Don't weasel out. I really need you here. Yes, or yes?"

My answer was automatic, directed by the needs of the Liberty Circle. What we needed was recruits, the wealthier the better, and a party at the Snowdons' would be fertile hunting ground.

"All right," I told her. "I'll catch the next bus and be there in an hour."

It wound up more like an hour and a half. By the time a white-gloved, rented butler admitted me at the door, my clothes were glued to my body. It was half past six already, but hotter than anything.

"He's here!" Lisa appeared at my side and threw her arms around me. She kissed me passionately, with no hint of her usual reserve. A second later, she pulled away in shock.

"Oh, my God..." She studied me for a moment, looking me up and down. "Have you been sick or something?"

I blushed. "I had the flu at camp," I said. "It went away. I'm better now."

"You look like a bread stick. A pale one."

"Lisa!" Her mother waved from the French doors leading to the back yard. I thought for sure she'd be annoyed—I wasn't exactly on the guest list—but she barely acknowledged my presence. She barely ever did. "Lisa, come here, dear. There's people I'd like you to meet."

We passed through the doors to a fantasy world where no expense had been spared. The Snowdons' meticulous yard had been transformed into a fiesta. A buffet straddled a deck by the pool, highlighted by Japanese lanterns. Beyond it, couples danced on an endless lawn. Smoke plumed from the grills past cages of purple light where insects burst into sparks. And, of course, there were people: white-gloved, jewel-encrusted rich people, posing at one another like Christmas trees. Their laughter competed with the music of a Dixieland jazz band. At least, I think that's what it was. It was a bunch of guys blowing on trumpets and stuff, anyway.

Mrs. Snowdon promenaded through the crowd, dragging us along like reluctant freight cars. I shook hands with two city councillors, a member of the Legislative Assembly, and the owner of the biggest mall in town. Once, pointing me out as "a resident of the downtown core", she went into an extended spiel on urban renewal. I stood and smiled benignly. She didn't know what she was talking about, but I was above getting angry now. I was a part of something better. I wouldn't grit my teeth and fume, the way the old Corey would have done.

Lisa finally broke us away and steered me back to the house. "Sorry about that," she said. "I know how you hate being round moneyed old farts like those. The youth contingent of this so-called soirée has stationed itself indoors. Follow me."

We entered the huge addition the Snowdons had added the year before. There was a second swimming pool here, one that shared the room with neon palm trees and a wet bar. The bar was open, too; it often was at these stiff little bashes, even for us kiddies.

I shook my head. "How do you get away with it?"

Lisa frowned, ever so slightly. "I don't know. Partly that my dad trusts me, I guess. Or maybe he's a bit naïve. As for Mom..." She shrugged, and a note of scorn entered her voice. "What does she care? She's too busy saving the planet to worry about me."

"I thought saving the planet was *your* job."

"There's a difference," she replied. "I'm not in it for image."

"Alleluia! Our hostess returns!" Some yuppie-puppy jerk walked up and threw his arms round Lisa. "And who's this, the lucky guy?"

"Hello, Reinhold," Lisa replied—a bit too enthusiastically, I thought.

"Marsha and I are making shooters," he said. "Come on over and try my electric popsicle."

"Shooters? I'm *there!*" Lisa cheered up visibly as she headed back to the bar. "Come along, sweetie," she told me, "let's get pissed."

"Thanks. I'll just have a Coke."

"A Coke? A *Coke?*" She looked at me like I'd sprouted

an extra head. "Who do you think you're fooling? You always have more than that."

I shook my head. "Alcohol tears down the body. It clouds the thinking."

Reinhold laughed. "This guy's not really your boyfriend, is he? I think he's been going to Sunday school too long."

"He's not serious," Lisa said. "Corey. Lighten up, Corey, please. Have a drink. Have several."

"No. It's bad for you."

"Jesus." She snatched a shooter off the bar, something yellow and green. She tossed it back like an expert. "What are you all of a sudden, my conscience?"

I could see she was getting drunk. I could see also that she needed the guidance of the Liberty Circle. But I couldn't tell her yet. *Don't give yourselves away too soon, they'd said. Distance your beliefs from Camp Liberty.*

"Look," said Lisa, "don't dampen the festivities. A lot of people are here, some you've never met. Let me do the intros, and we'll save the sermon for another day."

So she spun around, and threw names at faces for me, until they all blended together in the bar's neon glow. Then suddenly she hit one that didn't blend at all.

I stopped and stared, for what must have been several long seconds. Leon Boyer was black, darker than diesel soot. And that name—a black Frenchman?

"Pleased to meet you," I said at last, allowing a note of reserved politeness to enter my voice. I shook the hand he offered.

"Yeah. Same here, I'm sure," Leon responded. He continued to smile, but a knowing coldness had entered his eyes. "Real nice meeting you," he added, and he drifted on. A moment later, he was meeting someone else.

Lisa continued to circulate, but there was a subtle change in the way she acted. As soon as she could, she drifted away from her friends and pulled me out into the yard. Now there were darts shooting from her eyes.

"Why did you do that?" she demanded. "Why did you wait so long to shake Leon's hand? Do you know how he took that?"

"I was...surprised."

"By what?"

"The fact that he's black. There aren't too many in this part of town." Without thinking, I added, "Fortunately."

"'Fortunately'?" I watched Lisa's face go through an amazing series of changes. She finally settled on puzzled, and said, "What do you mean, 'fortunately'?"

I hadn't meant to let it out so soon. We weren't supposed to talk about our new beliefs for at least a month after camp. But now that I'd started, I knew I'd have to continue.

"Blacks are inferior to us," I explained. "In every way, shape and form. Aryans like you and me are the superior race. That's why most of the people in Harrington Gardens are Aryan. We're smarter, so we make more money. The only non-Aryans here are the Jews, who got their money by being deceitful. They control the banks..." My voice trailed away: Lisa's expression had gone from puzzlement to shock. Then, unexpectedly, she laughed.

"God, Corey, you are a tease. You really had me going. But I'm on to you now. You're joking."

"No." I looked her straight in the eye. "I'm not."

81

She regarded me closely for several seconds, then shook her head. "I don't believe this. Is this what they taught you at Camp Liberty?"

A chill seemed to pass through the yard, despite the heat of the day. I suddenly remembered advice I'd received in camp.

Think, they'd told us near the end of our stay, *of what would happen if the conspirators found out what we are doing? They would destroy us. They would have us brought before the courts on trumped-up charges like 'promoting hatred'. Us, promoting hatred! Promoting the truth, they mean. And the truth is their enemy...*

I shook my head. "I didn't get my beliefs from Camp Liberty. I've had them for a long, long time. All we did up there was learn how to live in the wild. I meant every word I said, though, about races that are inferior. And I could prove to you that I'm right."

Lisa said nothing. She looked beyond me instead, at someone in the cluster of people who had spilled out to see what was happening. I turned and saw Leon Boyer. He stood motionless, directly behind me, his eyes stonily fixed. In my Circle-induced mind-set, I actually saw myself as triumphant and him as publicly disgraced.

"I think," said Lisa quietly, "I'd better get you home."

I turned back to her, surprised. "Why?" I asked. "What's wrong?"

"You're acting really strange. It's like you're someone else." She turned on her heel and started for the garage, leaving me little choice but to follow. I thought I heard someone snicker behind me.

Too much, I thought, getting into Lisa's car. I gave too

much away too soon. And Lisa shouldn't be driving. I loosened the tie I'd worn, then took it off entirely. "I didn't want to hurt you," I said, "only to show you the truth."

She didn't answer. We made the trip downtown in silence.

When we got to my place, she wouldn't even let me kiss her. "Just go inside," she said. "Get some rest, Corey. I think you need some sleep."

I was left on the sidewalk in front of our building, watching the little car speed off into the night. I wondered how long it would take Lisa to get over being angry.

I really wanted to warn her about the conspiracy.

Nine

The next day was hotter still and completely without a breeze. The air over the city stayed where it was as a greasy yellow smudge. It reeked.

I trudged down the steps to Captain Nemo's, my mind in a smog of its own—but not because of the heat. Mom had discovered me home this morning. She'd nearly freaked over how thin I was, and I hadn't expected that. I hadn't expected her to notice, much less fret for a quarter hour. I hadn't expected her to care.

And I'd got some information from her—something I guess I'd once sort of known, but had chosen to forget. Information about Neil's family. See, Mom and Mrs. Haymond had hung out together once, when Neil and I were little.

The air-conditioning in Nemo's snapped me back to what I was doing. I stood in the neon blue and took a look around. Immediately, my hopes fell: Neil was there already, engrossed with some machine. Brother Keith was there, too, along with a number of other skins. I no longer winced when I saw them, of course. The Brashboys were friends now, allies in the fight to save the world. But that wouldn't make this easier.

Ranji was there. He glanced up from behind the counter, and gave me a sort of uncertain welcoming smile. I just stopped and stared at him coldly. A paki, taking a white man's job! I knew the whole story now.

Neil had spotted me. He waved and stood waiting by the machine with that happy, stupid, puppy-dog expression. I walked to him slowly, feeling the gaze of my fellow Aryans. Damn—why did so many of them have to be there? With all of them watching like that, there could be no mercy shown.

"Corey-of-the-forest returns," cracked Neil, turning back to his machine. "Want a game of doubles?"

"No."

"Suit yourself." He popped in a token and reached for the controls. "So how was Camp Liberty? Was it as weird as they say?"

"Who said it was weird?"

"Some friend of my cousin. I told you about that. His girlfriend went there, but she got sick and left a couple of days later. She said they played a lot of soldier games or something."

"Do you know her name?"

"No, why?"

Brother Keith drifted into my field of vision, passing beyond the video machine. Neil must have seen him, too, because he immediately flubbed his game.

He shook his head and put in another token. "I thought he was going to unplug it," he said. "Those guys have been on my case all day. There's something wrong with that bunch."

"There's nothing wrong with them," I said.

"Since when?"

I brushed a trembling hand across my face. "There's something I have to tell you." I couldn't put it off, though every muscle in my body was tensed. The others were waiting to hear it.

"Don't tell me," Neil said. "You're pregnant."

In another time, that would have broken me right up. I might have smiled now had I not felt more like crying. But those days were over for good. Taking a deep breath, I forced out what had to be said: "We can't be friends anymore, you and me. We never should have been."

Neil grinned, not missing a point in his game. "Okay. Why not?"

"Because you're a Jew."

His hands froze, and the machine made an electronic dying sound. Game Over. There was a few seconds silence, then, "That's not too funny, Corey."

The Brashboys were watching. "You see me laughing?" I said.

He turned to me slowly. The expression on his face said he knew I wasn't joking. "I think," he said cautiously, "you've been in the woods too long."

"That's got nothing to do with it. It has to do with stuff I've been reading."

Neil's eyes widened. "Hate literature!"

"No. I've been reading about the truth. You Jews are trying to take over the world. You already control the banks."

He stared for a few seconds, then laughed. "You're crazy." He turned back to the machine, but made no move to start it. "You're absolutely crazy."

"Your father was like that," I said, presenting my trump card. "He tried to get out of debt by burning down his store. He's in prison now, isn't he, Neil? Paying for his attempt at fraud..."

"*Shut up!*" Neil swung back to me with rage on his face, something I'd never seen in him before. "Just shut the hell up!"

For a moment, I did just that, his anger was that unexpected. Then I got a little mad myself. What if the Circle was right? What if I was seeing the real Neil, someone who'd been leading me on all my life? What if he was really just a conniving little Jewish creep, someone who couldn't care less about anyone but himself?

Anyhow, the Liberty Circle could never be wrong.

"You're just like your father, aren't you?" I said. "You're going to be just like—"

Neil hit me.

Five guys got a grip on him before he could do it again. "Whatta we got here?" a skin demanded, yanking Neil's head back. "A loudmouthed, uppity little kike!"

Behind the counter, Ranji stood up. "What is going on there, please? Let him go, please."

"Snap it shut, paki," Brother Keith growled. He followed as they dragged Neil out of the arcade and onto the stairwell. They threw him down there and knocked him about a little, I guess, while I stood and watched through the blue-tinted windows. Why were they doing this, I wondered? Hadn't I hurt him enough already?

Neil finally managed to roll away, nose bloodied, and get unsteadily to his feet. The last thing I'll remember is his eyes, the way they looked at me through the glass, blazing with anger, fear and hurt. Then he staggered up the stairs to the street, where he vanished into glittering, metallic heat.

Ten

E xcuse me, sir. Sir? Excuse me. How are you today? My name is Corey, and I represent the Effie Wagner Foundation. We're involved in sending needy kids to camp, and we're selling these delicious chocolate bars..."

The man in the sunglasses shook his head and strode off impatiently. I sighed and returned to the bench by the fountains where Julie waited.

"Have you noticed?" she asked cheerfully. "It's easier when you can make eye contact."

"It doesn't matter. We've reached our quota for today."

"Brother Corey! You know we aren't supposed to think like that! The quotas are only a minimum. Our goals should be much higher!"

"Yeah. I guess." I glanced down a corridor filled with Saturday shoppers. There was a family headed toward us, a girl my age and her parents. They were expensively dressed—and black.

"I think," I said with a smile, "I'll try those three over there."

Julie looked and lit up. "Go for it, Brother. It'll be a victory for Freedom."

I stepped out in front of the family and went into my

act. I had it down pretty good by now. "This Thanksgiving camp will be the last chance these kids get before cooler weather sets in," I concluded. "A lot of them have never escaped the urban rat race."

The black man chuckled. "Oh, do we have one of those?" But he reached into his jacket for a fat, black wallet, and thumbed out a couple of tens. "It sounds like a worthy cause."

"I'll match that," his wife said, and she forked over another twenty. "And please, keep the candy."

Then all three of us looked at their daughter, who cracked open her purse after a moment's hesitation. "Why not?" she said tartly. "And I'll take the chocolate."

I smiled as I took her five and handed her three of the bars. "Thank you," I told them. "This is very generous of you. God bless you all!"

The black guy waved "forget it", and the three of them continued down the corridor. I returned to Julie with forty-five bucks and a wild sense of achievement. "I don't believe it," I said. "Those niggers must be loaded."

Julie thumped me on the back. "That," she said, "was a classic, *classic* move. Well done, Brother Corey!"

I said nothing. I'd just spotted Lisa and one of her friends on the other side of the fountains. They'd been watching us, and from the expression on Lisa's face, I could tell they'd seen a lot. I handed my collection can to Julie.

"Lisa's here. I'll talk to her."

Julie nodded. "You know what to do."

Lisa whispered something to her friend, who made herself scarce as I approached. I tried to read Lisa's expression—puzzlement mostly, and maybe something like fear. She wore earrings that looked like crystal drops of water.

"Hi, babe," I said, genuinely happy to see her. "How're things going?"

"Fine." Her voice was flat. "Are you feeling better today?"

Instead of answering, I kissed her. It was like kissing an iron fence.

"Why are you selling chocolate bars? And who the hell is *she*?"

"We're collecting money for the Effie Wagner Foundation. They send needy kids to camp. Julie's on my canvassing team."

"Oh, really? You've never shown that kind of interest in anything before."

"This is different..."

"What about the time I wanted you to canvass with me for the United Way? You said you'd go door-to-door collecting money when you saw the devil wearing a tuque."

"This is different. It's not door to door."

"Oh, no! It's pestering people in a mall, which must be *much* more fun!" She glared at Julie, who was dutifully selling off the last of the bars. "You two seem like pretty good friends."

"But that's all we are."

"Really?" She reached into her purse and pulled out smokes. I thought she had quit. "So tell me," she said, lighting up, "do your friends at the foundation know about your beliefs? Like the things you said at Mom's party, about Jews and people of different races?"

"No. They don't."

"You don't really believe all that stuff, anyway. I mean, it was all just a sick joke, right?"

"It wasn't a joke."

She looked at me mournfully. "I heard something. Someone said you did something to Neil."

"Who said?"

"It doesn't matter. Is it true? They say you bloodied his nose, and he hadn't done anything to you."

"I didn't hit him. It was someone else."

"Keith?"

"No."

"That's not what I heard. I heard you two are real pals again. You haven't hung out with him in ages."

"I do now."

"What happened with you and Neil?"

"Nothing. I just can't be friends with him anymore."

Lisa sighed and looked away. "This isn't happening," she whispered. She lifted her cigarette with trembling fingers and took a lengthy draw. "I remember why I was first attracted to you. Partly, I think, it was to piss off my parents. But it was more than that. You were so tough, Corey, on the outside—a real streetwise, tough kind of guy. You were athletic. A jock. But I could see inside, too. You were different on the inside." She looked back at me suddenly and laughed.

"I know what this is," she said. "It just hit me why you've joined this Effie Wagner thing. It's because deep down, Corey, you know you really aren't a racist. Your subconscious went out and got you involved with a charity, to prove to you that you're not that kind of person." Her voice got strained. "I know you better than you know yourself, you dope. You don't really hate Neil. I happen to know for myself how gentle and caring you really are..."

She broke off, and looked at me as if waiting for agreement. Her eyes seemed suddenly moist.

Something moved in me then, something I hadn't felt since before camp. I could tell how she must feel. She and Neil and I had been friends forever, the Three Musketeers, a self-made support group. The world couldn't touch us whenever we got together. And I could see now how Lisa had needed those times at Neil's as much as I had. Like me, though maybe for different reasons, she needed an escape. And she was immensely fond of Neil.

I pulled her close. *Suppress your emotions*, they'd taught us—but not even Camp Liberty could kill what I felt for Lisa. She loved me. She needed me. And my heart was thumping like a leaky muffler.

"You must be Lisa! Oh, it's just so good to finally meet you—Corey's told me all about you!" Julie wedged her way between us, grabbing Lisa's hand like a long-lost sister's. At the same time, Lisa's friend materialized from nowhere. Any hopes I'd had of being alone with my girlfriend went flying down the corridor.

Julie took over the show. She told Lisa and her friend how we'd met, how I came to join the Effie Wagner Foundation, how she'd practically had to beat me over the head to help her canvass. She told them a lot of things, most of which were absolute bull. Slowly, Lisa's expression began to soften.

"There's just one thing I don't understand," she said

at last, crushing her cigarette under her heel. "You talk of making the world a better place with this foundation. What is the Effie Wagner Foundation, Corey? I've never even heard of it."

"It's fairly new," I said. "It's—"

"—an environmental organization," Julie put in. "We hold seminars on energy efficiency and solar heating. We collect trash along the riverbank. We give speeches in the schools. Right now we're collecting money for a 'nature camp' for needy children."

Even then, I remember thinking how incredible it was that Julie could pull this stuff from the air. And then came her grand finale:

"Next month," said Julie, "we'll be collecting to save the whale."

"The whale!" Lisa's friend peered self-consciously at Julie through a pair of granny-ish glasses. "I love whales. I love anything to do with the sea. Especially porpoises."

"No!" Julie put a hand to her forehead. "That's the month after!"

"That's uncanny," Lisa said. "Look, Darlene, you're even wearing the earrings I gave you. The ones that say 'Save the Whales'."

Darlene touched her ear. "I don't believe it. You must have seen them already, Julie."

"I didn't, though. I swear!"

And she looked so convincing that even I would've believed her, if I hadn't known better. She'd seen them, all right. And she'd taken a gamble, one that had paid off good: the earrings were a statement, not just decorations.

Now Julie drove it home, by telling Lisa and Darlene about a meeting Thursday night "at the home of a professor friend". It was open to the public, she said, and anyone interested in saving the globe was welcome. "It would be *just so good* if you could make it."

Darlene was fully hooked, though Lisa was a bit skeptical. It didn't take much more persuading, though—mostly out of me—to get a "yes" from her too.

Finally, after making me promise to call, Lisa went off with her friend. Julie and I left, too; mall security had found us again. It didn't matter. We had several hundred bucks in our pockets, plus a couple of possible recruits. And one of them was Lisa.

It had been, I reflected, a good day for the Cause.

We passed through the food court on the way out, where the noise and colour seemed suddenly depressing. Too long a ride on the merry-go-round, a carnival tune played out of key. I found myself chanting our slogans, just to clear my thoughts.

It worked. By the time we reached the parking lot, I had nothing on my mind at all.

Eleven

Neil was a problem. It began with school in September, when I realized we'd still be sharing the bus. See, we went to Lisa's school, not the one in the Flats. I'd got the idea out of self-preservation, and Neil had naturally followed. It's how I'd wound up meeting Lisa.

You don't get choice of public transit between the Flats and Harrington Gardens. What you get is the Number Six bus, and not a whole lot else. And that was going to be awkward.

But we caught it at different stops, and sat nowhere near each other. He didn't say anything. He never even looked at me. And that was the real problem. Jew or not, he'd been my best friend all my life. Now it was like I didn't exist.

He was an even bigger problem the morning after I'd carried out a new assignment. I hadn't intended to be there, not really; I just happened to round the corner as Neil was opening his locker. But I stayed, foolishly, to catch his reaction when he saw what was in it.

There was no reaction. He picked up the leaflet listlessly, read a little, then turned and looked straight at me. He hadn't seen me enter the corridor—he just figured I'd be there. And like an idiot, I was, if only by accident. I might just as well have walked up to him and said, "Hey, kike, what do you think of the literature I put in your locker?"

I went to class feeling miserable, but cheered up as the morning went on. The leaflets were causing a stir. I'd placed over three hundred the night before, and by morning break, the entire school was talking about them. The principal prowled the halls in a rage. The school newspaper got on the case. It was all I could do to keep from showing the elation I felt.

Lisa killed that elation at 12:04.

We met in the cafeteria as always, only she didn't smile when she saw me. She sat, pulled a leaflet from her lunch bag and slid it across to me. "Did you have something to do with these?"

"No!" I replied, working a defensive tone into my voice. I picked up the leaflet and examined it like something I'd never seen. "I heard something about it, though. What is it?"

"You tell me. They're everywhere. Someone stuffed them into half the lockers on the second floor."

"So? What makes you think it was me?"

"Read it. It seems to agree with your new beliefs."

I ran my eyes over the sheet, but my mind was on something else. She'd asked me to read it, and that could mean only one thing: she didn't believe I was responsible. Or she didn't want to believe.

I wanted her to believe what was in the leaflet, though. I wanted her to know how real the conspiracy was, how soon it could steal our freedom. "I've never seen these before," I said. "But what it says makes a lot of sense."

Lisa blew air from the corner of her mouth, displacing a strand of hair. "Corey," she said, "get real."

"No, look. This shows *proof* that the Jews never died in World War Two. Not six million, anyway."

"It's a piece of garbage."

"Have you read it?"

"Enough to know that it's a piece of garbage."

"But you haven't read it."

"*No!* Corey—" She covered her eyes for a moment, embarrassed at having raised her voice. "Give it to me. I'll put it down the toilet."

"No. I want to read it." I stuck it into my pocket.

Lisa shook her head. "You're changing, Corey. You are turning into someone else. You don't get involved anymore. You won't go for track. You've stopped going to parties. You aren't even painting. You haven't got time for anything but running around selling chocolate. I'm still convinced some...cult...has a hold on you."

"It's not a cult."

Lisa blinked. "*It's* not a cult? *It's* not? What is *it*, Corey? There is an *it*, then, isn't there, something you've got involved in? Something to do with that 'Effie Wagner Foundation' thing. Something to do with that camp."

I held up a hand to tell her to wait until I could wolf down a mouthful of burger. What I was really doing, of course, was thinking of something to say. "Don't do that," I said at last. "Don't make me laugh when I'm eating."

"What's so funny?"

"You. Someone made a racist joke at camp one day,

and Gunnarsson nearly smacked him. And you think he has something to do with this."

"I never said that."

"He's connected with Camp Liberty, which you connected with my beliefs, which you connected with those leaflets."

Lisa stared at me a moment, then shook her head. "Screw it," she said. "Just forget I said anything, okay? Are you taking me to that dance?"

"Yes."

I didn't. It was at one of the coolest night-clubs in town, one that was having a "teen night". She'd asked me about it before. But two days before it happened, the Circle scheduled a meeting. It turned out to be important. A man had come up from California to warn us of developments there. Things were worse than we thought. The Aryan race was in danger like never before.

I wanted Lisa to know. She had to be part of our struggle, part of the force that would lead us to Freedom. When we won the war against the conspirators—and we would—I wanted her there with me.

If only she'd come to another meeting. She'd been to the one, at Liberty Hall, and had promised to return. She never had. We were having better luck with Darlene, but I was certain we could still get Lisa. If she'd just sit down and listen to me, I knew she'd see the light. I wouldn't even mention the Liberty Circle.

It was Halloween before a chance came along.

I took her to a dance at our school, my evening planned in three parts. First, we'd spend some time at the dance. Later, on pretense of slipping out to talk to someone, Brian Taylor and I would blitz every locker in the school—our biggest effort yet.

I was getting pretty good at it now, having done Harrington twice and three schools on the west end once each. What's more, people were starting to listen. Brian, for example. He wasn't a part of the Circle—had never even been to a meeting—but he believed the same things as me. A promising recruit.

Part Three would come when I got back to the gym. Lisa would be ticked off—I'd be gone for half an hour—so I'd take her somewhere to make up for it. We'd sit in Pizza Hut stuffing our faces, and I'd tell her about the conspiracy.

Kids were already dancing when we got there; I guess you lose your inhibitions earlier when you're in costume. Lisa took a look around, saw where she wanted to sit, and dragged me over by the ears.

"This is stupid," I said, adjusting my bunny suit.

"Don't feel so bad," said Lisa. "Look what Neil's wearing."

I did and decided things could be worse. He was with Joyce Hughes, the girl he'd been going with lately. She'd gone as Raggedy Ann, so naturally he was Raggedy Andy. He was wearing a floppy red wig and this ridiculous costume, right down to a pair of socks striped red and white. There was make-up on his face. The effect was not too tough, if you know what I mean.

I looked away in disgust. "Big deal. It suits him, anyway."

"Remember last year? The two of you came as a zebra."

"He got the back end. It was very appropriate."

"Why don't you go over there and talk to him? He probably isn't even mad at you any more."

"Like, I care?"

"Like, you do." She stared at me with pleading eyes, and for an instant, I wanted to do just what she suggested. Only I couldn't. Not now, and not ever.

Then the band struck up an ancient classic—"Twist and Shout"—and I got up and pulled Lisa from her chair. "Come on," I snapped. "Let's boogie." I led her across the floor until we were smack in front of the speakers. At least there she had to shut up about Neil.

We danced for a while and hung out with kids we knew, and all the time I kept looking about for Brian. He'd told me he'd be dressed as a hunchback. His hunch would be full of leaflets.

About an hour into the dance, there was a commotion at the entrance. Lisa looked first, and her eyes narrowed. "I don't believe it," she said.

I turned and saw one of the local jocks, his face and arms painted black. There was a noose around his neck, and a watermelon under his arm. Beside him, someone in a Klan outfit held the other end of the rope. They were trying to get past Mr. Bunt, the phys-ed teacher, only he wasn't having any: "I said, get *out!*"

"Please, massuh," begged the jock gleefully, "let's me stay, please, suh. Ah, begs you, this man wantsa *kill* me!"

But as anyone knew, you didn't screw around with Bunt. In a single, smooth move, he swung both of them toward the door. A moment later, they'd be ejected physically.

Except before that could happen, a dark figure strode toward the entrance. Howard Lincoln was the biggest guy on the track team—and one of the biggest blacks at Harrington. He put a hand on Bunt's shoulder. "Excuse me, Mr. Bunt."

Bunt didn't move. "Sit down, Howard," he said.

"Yeah," echoed the guy in the Klan outfit. "Sit down, *nigger*."

In the next moment, Bunt went flying and Howard had the guy in the sheet by the neck. He started pounding him, screaming at him, and then the other jock jumped in, then Mr. Bunt, and the next thing you know there were twenty guys in there at once, tearing the place apart.

I watched with a lurid fascination, like looking at a train wreck I'd personally caused. The whole school was getting into it! People were starting to listen! If we could capture that hostility, direct it somehow...

Four more teachers materialized out of nowhere. They helped take the fracas apart, one person at a time, but not before the glass entrance was shattered, along with one or two faces. There was a pause, a time of wondering whether the dance would continue, then all the guilty parties were shovelled outside. The music began again. That's when I spotted Brian, gesturing from the bleachers on the mezzanine.

The people at our table were babbling about what had happened. The momentum was building, I thought...and I was about to take it higher! I touched Lisa's shoulder. "I'm going to talk to Brian. I'll be back in a while."

She nodded to tell me she'd heard and returned to her conversation.

There were just a few kids in the bleachers, and the lights were off up there. It was easy to leave unnoticed. I led

Brian behind the seats. "I snuck in here right after school," I whispered. "I left this door ajar. Hold your breath."

It opened. We slipped through it quickly and let it shut behind us, locking off the rest of the world. We were alone, in a maze of semi-lit corridors. "Let's take off our shoes," I said.

Picture a large black rabbit and a hunchback padding through a school at night, sliding leaflets through vents in locker doors. It was hard to keep from laughing. There were other reasons to laugh, too. After the first couple of times I'd done this, it had made the city papers. The third time, a school board meeting. The fourth time, they had vowed to increase night-time security in every school in the city—though I didn't always strike at night. I hadn't noticed too much security the fifth time, and now Brian and I would make it an even half-dozen.

We were about three quarters done when we reached the art room on the second floor. This part is weird: the corridor splits in two directions, goes around the room on either side, then joins together again at the other end. It's the one room in the building completely surrounded by halls. I gestured to Brian to take the hall on the right.

I worked my way round the left, conscious of the sound of my own breathing. I didn't like this part. There were too many blind corners. All it would take was one janitor...

There was a flurry on the other side: Brian had dropped his leaflets. I winced and held my breath, fearful someone would shout, would demand what we were doing there. All I heard was the thumping of socked feet—Brian scrambling to pick up his leaflets, no doubt.

I wished he'd keep the racket down.

I quickened my pace. We'd been gone thirty-five minutes already, and there was still that one short hallway on the third floor to do. Lisa would be furious. I reached the spot where the corridors joined again, and found no sign of Brian. "Hey," I whispered, "get a move on."

No reply.

I stood for a moment at the junction of hallways, waiting. And that's when I noticed the leaflets, still scattered all over the floor. Too late, I saw Brian farther down the corridor, gesturing desperately.

I ran, but didn't get far; a strong pair of hands seized me from behind. "*Freeze*," Mr. Bunt ordered. "Don't even *think* of running."

I did think about it, and decided it was best not to. For one thing, it might expose Brian, who had slipped away down the hall. When he was certain I wouldn't bolt, Bunt stood me against the wall. I must have been something to stare at, too, dressed like the Easter bunny.

Bunt stooped to pick up a leaflet. He opened it, read a little, and sighed. "This is not good. You actually believe this crap, Copeland?"

I just stood there, saying nothing. My mind was on something else.

What would I say to Gunnarsson when he found out I'd been caught?

Twelve

The corridor outside the Main Office reverberated with the sounds of the free. I sat inside on the edge of a chair, staring at the principal's round old face. It was easier than looking at my parents. Dad was as hunched over as the day he lost his job. Mom looked like she wanted a beer.

Mr. Olfert placed a meaty pair of hands on his desk and studied them dourly as he spoke. "We've done a lot of talking, your parents and I," he rumbled, "about your life at home. It seems it hasn't been the best for you recently.

"Your mom tells me she's had problems with alcohol in the past—and Marty is having them now. Things have been a little rough for you, have they not? What I'd like to know—" He shifted back in his chair with a tremendous squeal of leather. "What I'd like to know, Corey, is have you ever wished you didn't live at home? Have you ever considered getting away for a while?"

I shrugged. "I guess that's right."

"Perhaps it would be easier if we spoke alone." Olfert glanced at Mom and Dad.

"No. We can talk in front of them."

"You don't mind?"

"I don't care."

"I see." Olfert pushed himself forward again. "Corey...you went away for a time this summer, did you not? A camp up north, for three weeks?"

An alarm went off in my mind. "Yes," I said cautiously.

"Did you enjoy yourself?"

"Sure."

"Did it help you to be in that environment? Or did you wish it had been different, that you had gone somewhere else?"

He's looking for something, I thought. *He's definitely looking for something.* "I liked it fine," I said.

"What did you do there?"

"I don't know. Camp things. We went swimming, canoeing, backpacking. We learned stuff."

"Ah." Olfert threw another glance at my parents. "What sort of 'stuff'?"

"How to saddle a horse. How to paddle a canoe. How to clean up the cabin." I looked him square in the eye. "Camp things."

"Nothing else? The advert mentions 'taking control of your world'...'the moulding and reinforcement of new ideals'...'how to deal with the forces threatening your freedom'."

"Oh, that. Well, there were lectures in the mornings. It was just sort of a...a social awareness thing. It was like camp with a little bit of school thrown in." I smiled at him like a sweet little kid.

He smiled back, briefly. "What kinds of social awareness did they concern themselves with?"

"Well, like getting along with your fellow man. Working to make the world a better place. How to solve problems like crime and starvation." An idea came to me, and I laughed out loud.

Olfert grinned. "What is it?"

"I was just thinking about the first lesson I had there. I got into a fight with one of my cabinmates the very first day. Peter Gunnarsson—one of the counsellors—broke it up. That's when I got my first lecture."

"What was the fight about, Corey?"

"I guess I called the other guy a kike."

Olfert's eyebrows shot up. "What happened then? After the fight, I mean?"

"Mr. Gunnarsson gave me that lecture. He said the camp was for everyone, and to keep my opinions to myself."

"I see. So you didn't form any of those opinions during your stay at Camp Liberty?"

I gave him a look like it was a really strange idea. "No."

"Where, then?"

"That's my business."

"*Corey*!" Dad sat up in his chair, his face crimson. He looked like he wanted to thump me one right there in front of the principal.

Olfert waved a hand, a gesture that said "forget it". When he looked back at me, though, there was a hardness in his eyes. "Are you aware, Corey, that you have broken the law? That we could have you charged, probably for three or four different things?"

I lowered my eyes and tried to look penitent. The main

107

thing here, I knew, was to protect the Liberty Circle.

Olfert began counting his fingers. "You've trespassed, six times..."

"Three. I told you, I only did the leaflets here, at Harrington."

"...six times, you've promoted hatred of the worst sort against minority groups, you've refused to even tell us who was working with you when you were caught... Corey, if we were to press charges against you for all of this, you would be in a very large amount of trouble. Do you understand this?"

"Yes, sir. But I did not do the ones on the west side."

"If you didn't, who did? The leaflets were the same."

"I don't know."

"Where did you get those leaflets?"

"I already told you that. A guy pulled up in a car one day and showed them to me. He asked me to spread them around. I didn't get his name."

Mr. Olfert sighed deeply. "Who are you trying to protect, Corey? Whose name are you afraid to give? Or is it a group?"

"Nobody. I did this myself, alone, except for the guy in the car. I'm telling you the truth, sir."

"If my son says he's telling the truth," Dad offered, "then he probably is."

I couldn't look at Dad at all after that. Whatever trust existed between us, I had just betrayed. But that's the way it had to be. The Liberty Circle came first.

A knock at the door exploded into the silence. Constable Stuart, the school liaison officer, stepped into the room.

"Corey," said Mr. Olfert grimly, "would you please wait outside again for a few minutes? Thank you."

I went out, and the door shut behind me once more. I sat in the chair and let the realization of what was happening wash over me like a wave. The whole leaflet campaign was collapsing, all because of me. And as for Lisa—she'd freaked when she'd seen me being led out that night by Bunt. She'd more than freaked when she'd found out why.

"How could you do this?" she'd practically screamed. Bunt was still holding on to me, just inside the front entrance of our school, and Lisa was there. Word had spread right to the gym, and she'd come with the crowd of curious—or maybe, the crowd of furious. Hard words got flung my way, along with a Coke or two. It could have turned into a riot.

Lisa had shaken her head and cried, the tears smearing her bunny makeup. "You jerk," she'd sobbed. "You jerk, Corey. You were one of them all along!"

I'd opened my mouth to answer, like I was about to try denying it. There wasn't any way to. She'd looked at me once again as the police cruiser pulled up, then walked away with her friends. I hadn't heard from her since.

And now I sat alone, listening to echoes from the principal's office. I closed my mind, gave it over to the chants.

A long while later, they called me in once again. Olfert and the cop did all the talking now. They said there might not have to be any charges. They said they were working their way around it, that the guy in the car who gave me the leaflets was the one they *really* wanted.

They said if it weren't for my perfect record—ten years of school without a problem—then things would probably be different.

"But, Corey," said the principal sadly, "we must take some action with you. The decision we have reached—your parents, Constable Stuart and I—is that you leave us for the rest of the semester. You may continue your education through correspondence courses, or you may wait until you join us again in February. In the meantime, you are to report once a week to the guidance office, once a week *without fail*, as a condition of returning to Harrington Collegiate—or any school in the public system."

That was all he said, and then no one said anything at all. The principal's words hung in the air like a mist, sinking slowly into the wood. I was to speak next, it seemed. But the noon bell had pulsed through the walls and an airplane droned by overhead, and still they waited.

He had not said what he meant. He had not used the actual words.

"You mean," I said, my voice a creak, "I'm being expelled. And you're putting me on probation."

Mr. Olfert nodded. "It's better than having the justice system do the same, Corey. This way, you won't have a record."

"Yes." I didn't want a record. I hadn't done anything to deserve one.

Ten years. Ten years of school without a problem. And Jesus, oh, Jesus, what about my scholarship?

"There is one more thing," Mr. Olfert said, fidgeting with a pen. "You, ah, probably know that we have a shortage of lockers. A good many students have had to double up. We'll have to ask you to clean out yours and turn in your lock before you leave. We'll make new arrangements upon your return."

So that's what I did, while Mom and Dad waited in the car. I was grateful the noon hour was on, and that most students had gone to lunch.

On the way out, I stopped at the pay phones in the lobby and dialled Captain Nemo's. Gunnarsson was out. I'd have to catch him later, just as soon as I could. I needed a chance to explain.

I left school and got into the car with Mom and Dad. We rode in complete silence, all the way home.

When we got there, we had one hell of a fight.

Thirteen

I stepped onto Eleventh and paused, ignoring the chill of rain. Before me lay Electric Avenue, that kaleidoscope of neon bars where everyone who was old enough went cruising Friday nights. I'd never seen it like this: the streets were mirrors tonight, doubling everything. *Someday*, I might once have vowed, *someday I'll paint a scene like this.*

But "someday" was over, as far as I was concerned. It had ended at Camp Liberty on the morning of the squirrel, and wouldn't return until we'd defeated the conspirators. Nearly every spare moment I had was pledged to the Liberty Circle. Assuming, of course, I was still a part of it.

I had to be. They wouldn't just leave me alone in this mess, not after everything I'd done for them. They wouldn't abandon me to the conspirators because of one mistake. No. They couldn't. They were the only family I had. Especially now that Lisa was gone.

A breeze dug its way through my clothes, and I zipped my jacket higher. Those mirrors in the streets were turning to ice. It didn't matter; I had problems to deal with far worse than the cold of November. I turned and started down the alley to the rear of Captain Nemo's.

It was ten p.m., and I was exactly an hour late. It wasn't my fault. Dad had grounded me after our little "family discussion", and I'd had to sneak out down the fire escape. If he discovered me missing, he'd kill me. Assuming I lived through this.

The service door at Nemo's creaked open before I could reach it. I ducked behind a disposal bin and watched Ranji emerge from the arcade. He climbed the stairs to his quarters, peering nervously about—like he *expected* someone to be there. I caught a brief odour of exotically spiced foods, then his door was closed against the damp. Below, the window of Gunnarsson's office glowed dimly.

I slogged through the puddles to the service door, half-wishing I could stay out there. Three knocks on the door, a pause, then one more. Brother Allen admitted me, and it was hard to read his expression. He led me silently to Gunnarsson's office. A dozen Brothers and Sisters were there, at least half of them Brashboys. Everyone looked grim.

"Corey." Gunnarsson motioned me to his desk.

"I know I'm late," I began. "I couldn't get out of the—"

He cut me short with an impatient wave. "I've heard the story second-hand. Now let's hear it from you."

For the briefest moment, I hesitated. Who, I wondered, had he spoken to? And if our versions differed, which would Gunnarsson believe? But, no. Everyone here was an Aryan, as dedicated to the truth as myself.

So I told them everything, even about my scrap with

Mom and Dad. By the end of my little tale, Gunnarsson was nodding.

"I heard about your expulsion from school. I'm sorry it happened. Your education should be valued above anything, especially by a man in your principal's position. He is a fool. But at least you won't have to make a court appearance. That would have been bad, Corey, bad for you and for everyone."

I swallowed. "Yes, sir. I know."

"It's good that you know." He drummed his fingers on his desk, staring at me with that hardness you sometimes saw in his eyes. "Well...we've lost a golden opportunity, haven't we? The opportunity to spread word of the Truth to hundreds of young people—to win them over to our way of thinking. But it had to happen sooner or later. In fact, I'm surprised it's gone on this long."

I blinked and looked up at him. What was he talking about? He expected this to happen?

Gunnarsson suddenly smiled grandly, like God dealing out forgiveness. "It's okay, Corey. You did well, very well, to keep the Liberty Circle out of it. You also protected a possible recruit, by covering for Brian. You've done your duty, as far as the leaflets are concerned. Well done, Brother Corey!"

"Bravo!" someone exclaimed.

"You've saved the day," added another.

The hands and arms came, taking me in, taking me back. A moment ago, I could have sworn they were ready to knock me out. Now I was like a teddy bear in a little kid's arms. I felt safe again, safe as anything.

What I *should* have felt was pissed off at them, for

letting me sweat like that. I just didn't know it then.

When it was over—when Gunnarsson was certain that *forgiven* was all I felt—he went on to other matters. "We have a problem," he announced, "with our Pakistani friend upstairs. He came across some of our literature one day, while poking around in this office, where he has no business being. I'd have fired him on the spot, but I can't be certain he's never removed anything. If he has samples of our literature, he could give us serious problems—and I think he knows it."

Someone whistled. "You think he's part of the conspiracy?"

"He's not bright enough," Gunnarsson said, "to be part of anything. But he can be a threat. We need to give this lad a warning. Brother Chet, I'm putting you in charge of it. Nothing dramatic, you understand—just get the idea across. All right?"

"Yes, sir."

"One other little problem: Yannick Quisell. He seems disenchanted with the Liberty Circle. He has openly questioned our techniques, twice. He has too many things to say. And now he's missing meetings. I'd hoped our little session with him last week would solve the problem, but apparently it hasn't. What's more, we had him involved in some fairly sensitive areas. He could become a menace of the very worst kind. Brother Keith?"

"Yes, sir?"

"See to it that Yannick does not become a menace. Take whoever you need for help, and don't forget to keep me informed."

"Yes, sir."

"All right." Gunnarsson stood up, and his voice became a shade louder. "Not everything is a problem. Our park cleanup, for example. Thanks to the Brotherhood of Aryan Skinheads, there's not a scrap of litter left anywhere in McTavish Park. And thanks to their—" He smirked. "—their techniques of *gentle persuasion*, word has been spread that McTavish Park is not a good place for a non-Aryan to be. There has been public resistance, of course—but not as much as we feared.

"Credit our driving out the druggies and freaks for that. The business community loves it. Most of the park users love it. The ones that don't are lunatics from the fringe—or minority down-and-outers. No one listens to them.

"We've done it, bang on schedule. We've started an 'Aryan Zone'.

"And it doesn't stop here. That park is merely the beginning, a seed, nothing more. Our Leader has bigger plans for the Zone. Next, for instance, the shopping centre across from the park. If we can have an Aryan park, why not an Aryan mall? Then an Aryan business block, restaurant, night club—bit by bit, block by block, we'll build a mighty Aryan city! And there will be other cities..."

His voice carried us through the next hour and beyond, building a fever in us even as midnight came and went. He made us picture in our minds the images that bloomed in his own: a united, Aryan North America, where all lived in wealth and peace. He made us want it to happen one day. He made us believe that it would.

By the time we left, we were like a hyped-up family leaving a church—a family with a mission. But it was also a family where each person looked out for the others, where everyone hated to part. A family like I'd never known.

I'd started down the street when someone called my name. I turned and saw Keith and Dave.

"Remember that problem with Yannick?" Keith asked. "Gunnarsson said to use whoever was handy. I've decided to use you and Dave."

Fourteen

Yannick lived in College Hill, a fairly classy part of town. I mean, Harrington Park it's not, but anything beats the Flats. Keith drove us in his brother's car and filled us in on the way.

"He was doing good, really good. He only started when we did, and already they were talking about making him a camp counsellor. He could have done great things. But when he tried moving into Liberty Hall, his parents found out what was happening. They 'showed him the light' or something. They've got Yannick totally brainwashed."

"Just like they told us," I mused. "'Deprogramming'. The worst they can do to you."

"It is." Keith shook his head and swore. "We've tried to reach Yannick a dozen ways, but he won't even talk to us now. He'd probably have a lawyer on our ass right now, suing us for 'misleading' him—that's happened before, you know—except he's scared. He's one of those guys who's basically scared of everything. Mostly he's scared of what we'll do to him if he gives us any trouble. And that's what we're up to tonight—reminding him what could happen if he screws us around."

Beside him, Brother Dave nodded slowly. Dave had been a skinhead long before camp, long before the Brashboys merged with the Circle. Like so many in the Circle, he seemed unnaturally quiet. "If he's scared of everything," he muttered now, "he can be kept out of our way easily enough." He stared out at the sleeping streets gliding by. "Fear is an enormous weapon."

Keith shut off the lights and cruised to a stop round the corner from a quiet crescent. He shut off the engine. "Scout it out, Brother."

Dave got out and disappeared into the alley. I looked at Keith for an explanation, but he seemed to have developed a sudden interest in sorting gas coupons. What was going on? Had these guys been here before? Why did I suddenly seem to know so much less than them? Maybe, I thought unhappily, it was because of my screw-up with the leaflets. Maybe I'd better do something to try and make up for it.

Dave reappeared soon enough, sauntering out from the alley like someone on his way to a graveyard shift. "It's fine," he said back in the car. "No lights there or at the neighbours'."

"Good." Keith pulled something out from under the seat. "Let's go, Corey. Dave, you stay here and keep watch."

We got out and started down the alley. It was dark here; most of the yards were edged with trees. In the copper glow from distant streetlights, I made out a tree house, a trampoline, a child's swing set and slide. I wondered what my life would've been like if I'd been born around here instead.

I stepped on a frozen puddle, breaking through with a crash.

"*Shhhh!*" Keith crept up behind me. "This is it."

We ducked behind the fence and peered at the house through the slats. The place glowed dimly white, with black spaces at the windows. It looked like a giant skull. I shivered.

"What are we going to do?" I whispered.

"You are going to deliver a message. Hold out your hand."

I did, and he slapped something heavy, solid and cold into it. I squinted in the dark, and it was exactly what it felt like. A brick, with a note attached.

"The message," Keith said, a trace of laughter in his voice. "His room is on the second floor, last window to the right. I'll wait for you here. Don't get caught."

Don't get caught? No kidding! But there was no way I would back down now. If anything could prove to the Circle that I was still worthy of being trusted, this would have to be it.

The gate squealed as it opened. I froze in place, my heart revving. Surely there were eyes in every window, seeing me there with that brick. Then I spotted the floodlights below the eaves. At any given instant, the entire yard could be flooded with light!

But a sound from Keith prodded me on. I approached the house the way a prisoner would the gallows, my feet dragging in the frozen grass. Yannick's window loomed larger.

I stopped.

This is insane, I thought. It's illegal. Maybe Yannick is

right to question the Liberty Circle. Maybe all I'm doing is proving how right he is.

But you are an Aryan, a voice inside me reminded. *You know there is a conspiracy in the world. You know violence is necessary. And Yannick has become a threat. He must be brought around.*

My arm went back. I took careful aim, threw, and was running before the brick connected.

Glass exploded behind me, and a howl rose in the air. A dog, I thought at first—then realized it was an alarm. The floodlights came on. I whipped my jacket over my head and careered out of the yard, smashing my shin on the gate. Keith was a shadow at the end of the alley. He was getting into the car.

"*Wait!*" I stumbled after him, fell, rose to lurch forward again. A door slammed somewhere behind me. Voices began to shout. Lights came on in other houses.

They waited—just long enough for me to get one leg and arm in the car. Then we were off, the car spinning round icy corners as Dave reeled me in the rest of the way. We got onto the freeway, and off again. Only then, in another district, did Keith slow down the car.

He glanced at me disdainfully. "You nearly got caught," he said.

"It wasn't my fault," I gasped, clutching at my leg. "They had an alarm."

"Don't worry about it. I knew about the alarm."

I blinked. "You *knew*? Why didn't you tell me?"

Keith shrugged. He obviously didn't think it was important. "You hesitated, Brother Corey. Were you having Doubt?"

"No," I said, and immediately wondered why I'd lied. Maybe it was easier than getting into a big explanation, especially while I was in this kind of pain. If I had Doubt, I could always do the chant later.

He looked at me again, closely. "Are you all right?" he asked.

"Yes. No. I'll be okay. I've maybe got a sprain."

"We could take you to a clinic."

"Forget it. I'm fine."

So they drove me back to the Flats, at three o'clock in the morning. It was only as the car roared away that I realized the impossibility of reaching the fire escape in my condition. Worse, I'd forgotten my key. If Dad found out I was gone...

I looked up at our apartment. Only the kitchen window was lit. Marty? I'd have to take my chances.

So I limped around to the front of the prestigious Princess Anne. There was no lock at all on the main entrance; it had mysteriously vanished a couple of years ago. I staggered up to our apartment, buzzed short and sweet, and prayed.

I was lucky. Marty answered, and did a double take when he saw me.

"Corey-boy! What the hell're you doin' out here?"

"Cruising chicks," I snapped sarcastically. "Are you the only one up?"

"Just me n' Val." He glanced at his watch and whistled. "Jesus! You get yourself laid or somethin'?"

"Or something." I lurched into the hall, noticing only now the mud all over my clothes.

Marty noticed it too. "What happened?" he demanded,

an edge to his voice. "Some jerk go and jump you?"

"It's nothing, all right? I'm going to bed. You never saw me."

"Need any help?"

"Not from you, thanks. You look like you can barely walk yourself."

Marty grinned. "I had a coupla Blues," he admitted, which I took to mean "a coupla six-packs". He seemed almost proud to admit he was tanked up once again.

I entered my room and eased from my clothes, trying not to disturb my leg. By the time I got into bed, I was in agony from knee to foot. Sleep was out of the question. As if that weren't enough, there was soon noise coming through the wall from the living room: the sound of Marty and Valerie making reckless love.

Lying awake in the darkness, I tried to block out the world with the chant. For the first time ever, it didn't work. Something was wrong. I had hesitated tonight, when I should have acted without question. Was I really having Doubt? Didn't I trust the Circle? Why was I holding part of me back?

The money, for example. They'd asked us to give our all, including our bank accounts. A brother had accompanied me to the bank the week before, where he'd helped me close my account. I'd turned over forty-some dollars. No one knew about the withdrawal I'd made the day before that. There was a little metal box in my closet, containing almost five hundred bucks. That was for college, and not even the Circle was getting that.

Except we were never to lie to the Circle.

Something was definitely wrong.

Fifteen

A pounding at the door smashed into my sleep. "Corey, get the hell out of bed! It's past eleven o'clock!" Dad's voice, like thunder through the wood. But when I swung myself out, pain surged up my leg; it was all I could do to keep from crying out. I sat back on the edge of my bed.

The door burst open and Dad strode in. His face was the colour of fire. "When I tell you something, mister, I expect—well, what the hell happened to you?"

I glanced down at my leg, seeing for the first time how swollen and bruised it was. No wonder it hurt! "I fell," I said lamely. "I tripped in the dark last night."

Dad smiled, a dangerous, knowing smile, I thought. "Terrific. There I thought I had one idiot for a son. Instead, I find I have *two*." He reached into the pocket of his jeans and pulled out a familiar, folded sheet. "I'm going to ask you something, kid, and I'd better get honest answers. I'm going to ask you one more time if you believe what it says in this thing."

I looked at the sheet. It was one of the pamphlets we'd been handing out the night I was caught. It told all about the conspiracy, from the black cops to the Jewish bankers. I'd believed every word of it then, and nothing had happened since to change that.

"I believe it," I said, "because all of it is true."

Dad crumpled the leaflet and tossed it onto my desk with a curse. "This is my fault, you know. I left too much of your upbringing to your goddamned mother."

"I didn't get my ideas from Mom."

"I know that. What I don't know is, where *do* you get your ideas?"

"I get them from me. From reading the paper and watching what's on the news."

"According to this crap-sheet, all that's supposed to have been censored."

"It is. But you can see through it if you look real close. It's real, Dad. It's all absolutely real."

"Where'd you get those sheets?"

"You asked me that before. Like I said: some guy drove up one day and asked me to give them out."

"Did he pay you?"

"No."

"I've worked with Negroes, you know. Blacks. Side by side every day, on the same construction sites. They bust their humps like everyone else."

"It doesn't change anything," I replied. I wished he would understand.

For several seconds, he stared at me hard. "You're always like this—every time some club, some group, some *gang* comes along, you get sucked right into it. Peer pressure pretty much does what it wants with you."

He turned toward the door. "Get dressed and get out here," he snapped. "We're having an early lunch." He left the room, leaving no chance to argue.

I dressed quickly and hobbled to the kitchen, an uneasy feeling in my gut. Only yesterday, when the principal had doubted my word, Dad had stood up for me. Even during the family fight that followed, he was more ticked off at Mom and himself than me. This morning something was different. Something had changed, but I couldn't guess what.

At the table, weirdness was the order of the day. Valerie was silent for once, and Marty kept glancing at me on the sly. His expression was unnaturally serious. Mom buzzed round the table, making sure everyone was enjoying their meal. It was like she was trying to smooth things over after last night's battle, something she never did. She'd only do that to prevent one...

I looked at Dad. He was reading the morning paper, an unhealthy smirk on his face. I turned back to my meal and waited for the other shoe to fall.

It didn't take long.

I had finished lunch and was limping for the door when Dad's voice jumped out from the paper: "Where you going, bright-ass?"

Mom's weary sigh filled the air behind me. I turned, and saw Marty and Valerie sink a bit in their chairs. Dad set aside his paper. He leaned back and stared at me, his eyes like nails.

"I said, where you going?"

"Out. I thought I'd go to the employment centre and see about a job. Since I don't have school, I mean."

"A job." He sneered. "I got a job for you, bright-ass. Go look in the hall."

I did, and knew instantly I was in a world of trouble. With the pain from my leg the previous night, I must have just forgotten. I hadn't thought about the mud from the alley—but there it was, all over the floor. And at the end of the little trail of gravely soil and leaves, my shoes, caked.

I heard a familiar jingle behind me, the sound of Dad removing his belt. I hadn't had this now for nearly a couple of years. I'd been too old for it then and definitely was now. That didn't matter. What mattered was that I remember to show fear. It would be a lot worse if I didn't.

"You left this place," Dad snarled, "after I grounded you. You *defied* me. I work my goddamned ass off for you people, every chance I get, and this is how I'm rewarded."

"Dad," called Marty from the kitchen, and I had to admire his guts, "Corey's not so bad. Lots of kids—"

"*Lots of kids don't bite the hand that feeds them!*" Dad roared. "*And you shut your freakin' hole, or you'll be next!*" Turning back to me, he added quietly, "I'm going to fix you, Corey. I'm going to make sure you know what's what."

And then the first blow came, right across my backside. And it all came back to me, what that sting felt like, everything it stood for. I remembered the humiliation, the helplessness, the sense of being at his mercy. I remembered the fear.

The second blow came, across my thighs.

And the third, low across my back.

And the fourth, across my side now because I'd turned a little.

The fifth never came. I grabbed the belt before it could happen, and I looked him straight in the eye.

"Don't," I growled.

Then Dad went into a frenzy, reverting to his fists and slamming me against the wall. Blurred images spun through my mind: plaster falling into my hair, the world tilting at crazy angles as he propelled me back to my room, the floor rushing up to meet me. The door slamming so hard it cracked. My hand rising to my face to discover a sticky warmth.

After that I lay still on the floor, listening to a chair slamming into the sink, the apartment door crashing shut, my mother crying and Marty swearing softly. Outside, in the lot below my window, Dad's car screaming away. And then silence.

After a very long while, I stirred, to wipe the blood from my face. I got unevenly to my feet. I pulled a gym bag from the closet and threw in what clothes would fit. I didn't think of the cash in my closet. I could barely think at all.

I just edged out the window to the fire escape, worked my way painfully down it and left my family, I vowed, forever.

Sixteen

Oh, Corey..." Julie hugged me gently, mindful of my aching ribs. Her tears soaked into my shirt. "I'm so sorry for what's happened to you."

"It's for the best, though," said Allan beside her. "We'll be your family now, Brother Corey."

"Yes, we will!" Julie agreed. "We'll take care of you, and you can take care of us. Just think, to live and work with the Liberty Circle, on a permanent, full-time basis!"

"Welcome to Liberty Hall!"

They hugged me and shook my hand, Julie and Allan and the half-dozen others who'd come in from their work in the yard. My arrival here was an event, not something taken for granted like it would be at home. At home? This was my home now and would be from here on.

"Come on," said Allan, as the others returned to their work. "I'll give you the grand tour. Then we can assign you to something. I know you've been through a lot, but it's best to get back into the swing of things. It'll take your mind off your problems."

We stepped out the back door of Liberty Hall, a large brick house on a pleasant, tree-lined avenue. Someone had died, I'd heard, and willed it to the Liberty Circle—

or something like that. Details were hard to come by. It was a residence for members and a centre of many of our activities. It was used for recruitment dinners.

"This," said Allan with a sweep of his arm, "is our food production centre. Almost all the food you'll eat will come from here."

The back yard was all but gone. Tall cedars still grew along the back fence, and there were the remains of a deck even now being removed, but that was where normality ended. Most of the places around there were old, established, with pools and flower gardens. This one looked like a farm.

Square after square of ploughed soil lay before me, separated by watering pipes and hoses. There were at least three small greenhouses and as many garden sheds. Several Brothers toiled in the autumn light, readying the soil for next year's crop.

Allan beamed. "It took time," he said, "but we've done it. Everything here is done by hand—it's cheaper that way—but no one goes hungry. You see how we've trained plants to grow up those trellises? That conserves space for more. And the greenhouses extend the growing season. Come on—I'll show you where it goes from here."

We went back inside and entered the kitchen. This, too, had been pretty much rearranged: they'd knocked out a wall and expanded the kitchen into another room. As in the garden, appearances didn't seem to account for much. You could still see the scars along the floor and ceiling where the wall had been, and the added cupboards and counters didn't match.

The place was steamy as a sauna. A half-dozen Sisters

toiled at stove tops, boiling food in jars. One of them looked up and smiled.

"Like to try a pickle?" she asked.

I started, recognizing her at once. "You're Angie, from camp," I blurted. "The one who tried—" I caught myself just in time.

"The one who tried to escape," she supplied. "Yes. I was having great Doubt that day. But I'm better now, thanks to the love of the Liberty Circle! Please, Brother—try a pickle."

I did. I hadn't eaten since lunch, so I made that pickle go as far as it would. It was delicious, though I couldn't remember ever seeing pickles at Circle functions.

"We sell some of this stuff," Allan said, as if reading my thoughts. "We run a booth sometimes in the market area downtown. Maybe one of these days you can give us a hand with it. But for now..." He paused for a moment, staring at me. "Yes. I'll put you in the radio room. It's what Yannick was doing before he made his unfortunate choice. I think Brother Quinton is in there now. I'll introduce you, and he'll show you what to do."

I followed Allan up a flight of stairs, slowly because of my limp. At the end of a dimly-lit hallway, he stopped in front of a door. ENTER QUIETLY was scrawled on the wood in marker.

"This," said Allan dramatically, "is our radio room." He put a finger to his lips and swung the door open silently.

It was a private suite, consisting mostly of one large room—maybe servants quarters once. It must have been really nice around the time of Queen Victoria. Now lime green paper was shedding from the walls, revealing older layers beneath. The carpet was worn right through. The odours of mildew and rot combined in a stench like vomit. Through a door to the left, a toilet gurgled and chuckled senilely.

There was hardly any furniture, but there was a stereo you wouldn't believe. It covered a set of shelves that stretched along one wall. You didn't have to be an audiophile to realize this was something pretty cool. For starters, there were two of everything: two tape decks, two disc players, two amps. There was a mixer, too, and some equipment I didn't recognize. Nearby, an old TV groaned under the weight of a pair of VCRs. There was a microphone on a stand, and countless tapes and discs.

In front of it all was Brother Quinton, short and squat and pale. He glanced up when we entered, and I almost smiled—he looked like a jack-o-lantern.

Allan gave him his instructions, then quickly left the room. As soon as the door was closed, Quinton heaved a mighty sigh.

"All right," he said. "This'll take a while." He looked about for a moment, as if wondering where to begin. When he looked back, a spark of enthusiasm had entered his eyes.

"I had this idea," he began, "of a way to spread our message. It's a sort of pirate radio station. We play music, and do radio skits. We have all sorts of features. We fill the gaps of whatever the real stations aren't playing. We get sort of a—a cult following, and we never have commercials. And everything is screened for non-Aryan influences.

"And—" he snapped his fingers "—we have news, too, local and international—read the way it should be!

Brothers and Sisters of the Liberty Circle exchange reports from every city. It's a real network!"

I pointed to the VCRs. "We have a TV station, too?"

"I wish. No, what we do is we rent a lot of movies. We rent as many as we can, under all different names, and we sort of—change them. Instead of the end credits, the next viewer gets a video about the conspiracy. There's usually enough tape left at the end to do that."

Any normal guy hearing this stuff might have turned and left the room. I know *I* would have, before Camp Liberty. But not now. Now it just seemed logical, the proper thing to do, surreal as all of it was.

"This is great," I said, warming into it. "So am I going to be a disc jockey?"

Quinton looked wounded. "No. Maybe later. Mostly what we need you for now is driving. Have you a licence?"

"Almost a year now. Why?"

"We put a transmitter in this old beater we have out back. It has a stereo hooked to a transmitter—I set it up myself. You put in a tape, choose the frequency you want, and anyone in the vicinity can pick up what's on the tape." Unexpectedly, he grinned. "Guess where you park."

"Where?"

"Underground parking lots. They're dead radio zones. You tune to the frequencies of the most popular radio stations, and then when people drive in, suddenly we are all that they hear!"

I shook my head. "That's wild."

"There's more, too," Quinton added, his enthusiasm shifting gears. "A lot more. For example, you'll be responsible for distributing posters advertising our stations. And you have to learn how to dub tapes and work the equipment. For now, I'll teach you that..."

It took hours, though I hardly even noticed the time slip by. This was actually fun. They even had this campy technique of speeding up and slowing tapes, so you sounded like someone else. That way, Quinton explained, you could appear to have more announcers than you really did.

Allan had chosen my task well. For the first time all day, I was able to forget what had happened at home.

The days and nights that followed seem kind of a dream to me now; everything blurs together in no particular order. Most of what I can recall, I would rather just forget. Only I can't. Not that I haven't tried.

I ate poorly. They served little at Liberty Hall, not that I was often hungry. I didn't sleep much, either, and I did a lot of chanting. And in between all that were the "projects" of the Liberty Circle—designed, we were constantly reminded, to make the world a better place. The first one they involved me in was a test of sorts. It was a test I wish I'd failed.

"We have to know where your loyalties are," Allan explained one afternoon. "Mr. Gunnarsson may need you to play a key role in future programs. We need to know for sure that you haven't any doubts."

"I don't!" I protested, but Allan held up his hand.

"This is just a routine test, Brother, one everybody goes through. It's different for every person, but it doesn't mean a thing. It's only that we have to be sure. So...you will please see Brothers Tony and Keith after the evening lecture. Heil Hitler!"

A light snow began falling that evening just as the last blue light of day was pulling itself from the sky. By the time the "lecture" was over—another excuse for frenzied chanting—it lay inches deep on the ground. I found Tony glaring out at it from the kitchen's patio doors.

"It's bad," he griped. "It's so bright out there, we might as well be doing it by day."

Keith appeared at our side, armed with winter parkas. "Let's get it over with, Brothers. Things won't get better tonight."

We rumbled onto the freeway in a battered old pickup, wipers working furiously. I sat in the middle, waiting for my assignment in silence. No one had explained why Tony and Keith were acting like my superiors. After all, they'd only been introduced to the Liberty Circle the same time as me. Had they passed such a "test" already? Or was I still in the doghouse because of the leaflet campaign?

If I'd known what was coming, I wouldn't have gone along—not even with everything the Circle had taught me. Or maybe I would have. When you're convinced the whole world is plotting against you, you're capable of doing anything.

I got a hint of what was coming when we entered a neighbourhood not all that far from my own. I got another when Tony parked on a side street just two blocks down from Neil's.

"What's here?" I asked, feigning ignorance.

"You know," Keith replied darkly. He reached under the seat and pulled out something dark. "We each wear one of these. Put it on when I give the order."

He tossed me something that smelled like a potato sack. It was a hood, dyed black, with holes for the eyes and a rope threaded round the bottom. It looked like something an executioner would wear.

Keith was watching me with amusement. "Be sure you tie the rope," he warned. "Sometimes it tries to fall off."

I stared at him in amazement. "You've done this before," I blurted.

"A number of times. Why?"

"So you were in the Circle already—before Camp Liberty!"

He and Tony looked at each other and laughed.

"Don't look so stunned," Keith said. "There were several of us there among you. In your cabin, for example, there was Tony, Allan and Dave. They were there to help with the new recruits. Only half the 'freshies' were what they appeared to be."

I nodded, slowly, taking it in. Yes, that made sense, I supposed. Anything to further the Cause. "But why bother with Haymond? He's a puppy. He's no threat at all to the Circle."

"He's a *Jew* puppy," Tony snapped. "And our orders come from Gunnarsson."

"All right. Fine. So what do you want me to do?"

Keith laughed again. "Remember the squirrel?"

They got out of the truck without another word. I had no choice but to follow. I found myself reciting the chant to ward off unapproved thoughts.

We started down the alley to Neil's, and it was like walking on some strange planet. The city's light ricocheted from the falling flakes, chasing shadows from every corner. Our footfalls were muffled in icy feathers. Garbage bins squatted down the alley at intervals, black in the copper light. They looked like army tanks in rank.

"Put on your hoods," Keith growled.

We ducked behind the fence at Neil's, peering through the slats at the house. The back door light was off. There was one light on inside, down in the basement. Neil, probably, up late watching *Star Trek*. His mom and sister would be asleep, blissfully unaware of whatever was about to happen.

No, don't think about that. They're only Jews.

The gate creaked open softly, and Tony slipped through. He worked his way silently up the walk, stepping into tracks that were already there. He went right up the steps and reached for the light. Soundlessly, he loosened the bulb as much as he could. He didn't remove it completely.

He came back at double the speed, pausing only to shut the gate.

"Now what?" I whispered.

"Shhh. Now we lie and wait," Keith said.

I did what he said. About a minute later, he made a small, satisfied sound: "Bingo."

The back door had opened. Indian glided out, a low growl deep in his throat. I saw Neil, too, flicking the switch and staring up at the light. Burnt out, for all he knew.

He gazed around the yard, right to the back of the fence. I swore he could see us. I swore he could see me, right through the darkness, the hood, and all. But he looked away again, to the patio where Indian had taken to sniffing about in the snow. He pulled back into the house and shut the door against the cold.

"Perfect," whispered Keith. Beneath the hood, I felt, he was watching me intently. "Call the dog."

There was no need, as Indian had heard us there already. He let out a single bark as he trotted up to the fence.

"Shhhh. Indian, be quiet. It's me, Corey. Come here, old pal." I slid my glove off and stuck my hand through the fence. His tongue slobbered warmth onto my fingers. I heard the pound of a giant tail.

"Good." Keith reached into his parka and hauled out a plastic bag. "Feed him this," he said, and he produced a slab of beef—cooked, even. We were lucky to get meat for ourselves once a week at Liberty Hall.

"Here, Indy," I said, holding it over the fence. "Tonight's your lucky night."

I didn't know. I didn't know. I thought it was just an ordinary chunk of meat. I thought it was something to keep Indian busy while those creeps did whatever they'd planned. When they stayed there and watched as I fed him, I know I should have guessed. But I didn't. If I had, I wouldn't have done it. I would have resisted, even if they beat the crap out of me. But *I didn't know*—though Keith and Tony obviously thought I did.

We'd started back for the car, and still they hadn't done anything. That's when it finally hit me. Indian...that meat...

No. Oh, no.

The planet tilted, and I lost track of where I was. For

a moment, I thought I'd be sick. I tripped, I think, and felt myself sink in the snow.

"Get up, Brother! We have to keep moving! What's the matter with you?"

They yanked me out of the snow and dragged me along to the truck. We piled in and spun away, vanishing into the night. I struggled to remove my hood. "I'm okay," I breathed. "I must have a touch of the flu."

"You'll get a good night's sleep," Keith said, accepting my excuse without question. "The job is probably already done. That meat had enough strychnine in it to waste an elephant."

Tony glanced at me from behind the wheel. "You're okay with what had to be done?"

I thought of the way things were in the world, of how people were dying and wars were being fought because of the conspirators. I saw nuclear weapons aimed at me, people starving to death. I saw hatred, greed, sickness, everything going bad because of Commies and Jews. All the lies I'd been fed came back to me at once, and I believed in every one of them. I laughed out loud.

"No regrets," I said. "We acted because we had to."

But when we reached Liberty Hall, I had to break away to lock myself in the can. I'd done okay, I thought. I was an Aryan. I would help to free the world. It was only Doubt that was trying to defeat me, that was making me shake like this. I leaned over the toilet and heaved.

I am ill, I thought. I am sick, sick, sick.

Seventeen

T o our health." Brother Allan raised his drink, and glasses clinked together down the length of the table.

I drank deeply from my glass, enjoying the rare taste of genuine juice. Circle members normally didn't eat this well. Not that our food lacked nutrition or anything; it was a lot better than what we'd had at camp. It was just so *boring*. The good stuff was usually saved for recruitment dinners like this.

Lisa's friend Darlene sat beside me, shaking her head again and again. "There's so much love here," she said. "More love in one place than I've ever seen before. If only Lisa understood."

I reached down and squeezed her hand. "Maybe one of these days she will," I said. "Meantime, I'm glad you came. You're going to love Camp Liberty."

"We've got it all up there," Brother Paul added from her right. "We've got skiing, skating, hiking, maybe even ice-fishing if the lake's solid enough. And sing-alongs every evening, by the light of a roaring campfire!"

"If you like," I reminded her, "you can stay longer. And believe me, once you're there, you'll find it really hard to leave."

At the end of the table, Sister Julie stood and banged her glass with a spoon. "Everybody? Could I have your attention, please? Finish up those meals, campers—the bus will be leaving shortly!"

Beside her, Brother Allan raised his hands. "I know some of you hadn't intended on going—you'd only planned to come to dinner. I'd like you to know that if you've changed your mind, you're still more than welcome to come. All you really have to bring is you. We can supply the toothbrushes, parkas, mitts..."

"...and all the love you can handle!" chimed in Julie.

The recruits flocked into the parlour, where a guitar was already strumming. Behind them, a small army of Brothers and Sisters cleared the table in two minutes flat. When Sister Julie came back in, her face was flushed with excitement. "As soon as the bus leaves," she told me, "summon everyone to the church."

The bus got under way quicker than usual, travelling in the night like it always did now. That way, Allan had once told me, Camp Liberty's location would more easily remain a secret—protection from recruits that "didn't work out". When it was dark outside, it was hard to tell exactly where you were.

I went from room to room, spreading Julie's orders. I even woke the Brothers and Sisters of the "night shift". Within five minutes, everyone had their jackets on, and was heading out into the cold.

The church Julie referred to had just been purchased by the Liberty Circle. Now I understood the reason for the canvassing drives! It wasn't all that big, but it would suit our needs for a while. It held two hundred people.

We tramped toward it from Liberty Hall, just three blocks away. As we walked, we were joined by others: part-time members who lived apart, others coming in from assignments. We all arrived together, nearly sixty strong—and that didn't count those who were running the recruitment camp.

Inside, a half dozen Nazi flags covered the stained-glass windows. Above the pulpit hung a portrait of Hitler. A large-screen TV—another recent purchase—sat directly beneath it. We sat in the pews, expectant, all eyes on Julie, who had taken the stage. She waited for the room to quieten before she began, breathlessly.

"His name cannot be revealed," she said, "and only a few have seen his face. Even his voice must be disguised to protect his identity. But our Leader—he who built The Liberty Circle—will forge a new civilization. He will tear down the institutions built by the conspirators. He will create a new world order, a brand-new Aryan regime! Our Leader will truly be a Saviour, if we give him our everything. And—" she paused dramatically "—he has sent us a message. He will speak to us here tonight, directly to us on videotape!"

A cheer thundered through the room, as if we hadn't all been told of this earlier. As it died away, Julie suddenly looked grim.

"Before we view this message," she said, "we must remind ourselves of what we are up against." The screen beside her flickered to life, and someone killed the lights.

My stomach tightened as The Video From Hell played itself out once more. This was the video they'd shown us at camp, and many times since then. It was no less repulsive the hundredth time, but you still felt compelled to watch.

They'd changed it this time, added stuff. Screams and sounds that were worse than screams gushed through the speakers around us. If blood had a sound, this was it. I closed my eyes and tried in vain to shut it out.

It ended abruptly as always, with a sound like death. The lights came on, and this time it was one of the Brothers who was crying. Nearby, a Sister whispered a prayer to our Leader, as if he were some kind of god. Another had fainted.

"That's the way it is," Julie said, sorrow in her voice. "I'm sorry to have to begin like this, but it's important that you remember. So important." Then she clasped her hands together and beamed at us. "And now," she said brightly, "a message from—well, hello, Mr. Gunnarsson!"

We turned and saw him standing by the entrance. He was in full uniform. He threw his arm up in salute.

"Heil Hitler!"

"Heil Hitler!" we responded, a unified voice that shook the room.

He strode to the front, a gleam in his eye. He looked like he'd been standing there a while and had been pleased with what he saw. "Don't let me disrupt you," he said. "Please, continue with your meeting."

"Well..." Julie turned back to us, appearing slightly distracted. "The video. Our Leader has sent us a tape, made in a secret location. He is in his home in exile, where he can be guarded twenty-four hours a day. I don't need to remind you of the hardships he must undergo in the name of Liberty. You have all heard that he must be moved constantly, from one place to another, often unexpectedly in the dead of night. Many of the places he lives in are so primitive, they don't have indoor plumbing. The simple pleasures of life we take for granted every day are denied our very Leader! And why?

"Because we are Aryans! Because we stand for the Truth! Because we want to defeat those who would enslave us!"

A Brother leapt to his feet. "Smash the conspirators!" he cried.

"Free our Leader!" wailed another.

"Death to our suppressors!" And the chanting began in earnest.

"And now," said Sister Julie when it finally died away, "Brothers and Sisters, a message from our Leader!"

The lights went out and the TV lit up again. We saw a snow-capped range of mountains sliding across the screen. Mountains where? Mexico? Alaska? Alberta? This could have been anywhere. Then the camera pulled back and a gravely patch of land came into view. In the middle of that sat a figure in a chair.

It was impossible to recognize features; the face was blurred and indistinct, broken into digitized squares. "Brothers and Sisters," a reverent voice intoned from the speakers, "The Leader of the Liberty Circle!"

The camera zoomed in for a close-up, and the blurred figure opened its mouth. "My dear children," it began, "it is good to speak with you again."

In another time or place, I thought, this might actually have been funny; the voice sounded like a robot's, metallic and weirdly distorted. It was like many voices at once. But they'd had to disguise it for a reason, I recalled, and there was nothing funny about that.

"I am sorry to have to appear to you in such a cloaked form," the man continued. "I wish I could be with you now, with each arm of the Liberty Circle in every city, seeing and hearing and touching you. Yet, I am touched—touched by the countless stories of Aryan resistance that reach me daily. Touched by the efforts of all my children, each of whom makes personal sacrifices for the good of the whole. I am touched by a vision that grows stronger every day—the vision of a free world in which our struggles will have triumphed.

"Alas, that world is far off. As we redouble our efforts, so too do the conspirators. And there have been weaklings among us, Brothers and Sisters, who have let Doubt lead them away from Hope. Who have been brainwashed, 'deprogrammed', forced to turn us in. Yet we persevere."

He continued for another ten minutes, urging us to 'reach forever higher'. His voice had a grandfatherly quality to it, despite the electronic distortion. He spoke the way you'd expect a favourite uncle to. It was as if he truly did love us—like he wanted to reach out of the screen and give us all a giant hug. He was everything the Circle meant to us. He *was* the circle, in human form.

Looking back on it, it sounded as if he were reading from a script—a pretty melodramatic one. But of course, that's not how I saw it then.

The little squares on the screen changed as he moved, teasing the viewer with hints of his appearance. I found myself trying to place a face with the voice. His hair was grey, I thought—and was that a moustache? It was hard to say for sure. You'd no sooner think you had the picture when he'd shift again and the entire image would change.

"Remember," concluded our Leader, "I love you. I pray you will not let me down. Never forget that Liberty herself is balanced upon your shoulders. Please, serve her well."

And then this gentle, soft-spoken man raised a hand in farewell, and the screen faded to black.

The room buzzed as the lights came on, everyone blinking in the glare. Gunnarsson scanned the room from the stage, as if gauging each person's reaction. Julie clasped her hands and spoke solemnly.

"So you see," she said, "the sacrifices our Leader makes. We should all try to be so brave."

"Each and every day," Gunnarsson interjected, "we must do better than the day before. There is no room for dissenters, for those who won't give their personal best. You must be prepared to do willingly whatever is asked of you..." He went on like that, reminding us of things we'd been reminded of a thousand times before. I glanced aside for a moment—just to rub a cramp from my neck—and that's when I saw the skins.

The room was full of skinheads, of course, but these had entered in the middle of the Leader's message. They stood lined up across the back, arms crossed and faces grim. I counted six before the Brother behind me poked me in the ribs. I turned my attention back to where it belonged.

Gunnarsson was wrapping up. "The following Brothers of the Liberty Circle will please remain behind: Brothers Matthew, Corey, Tony, Brian and Keith. The rest of you may leave and return to your respective duties. Heil Hitler!"

It was hard not to feel important as everyone else filed out of the church. Small meetings like this were usually called to deal with some special project or problem. In the egalitarian world of the Liberty Circle, this was as close as you got to status.

The six skins I'd seen remained behind, making twelve of us in all. Gunnarsson locked the doors and shut off all the lights but one, a red spotlight over the stage. We sat down before him like disciples, cross-legged on the icy floor.

"The goddamned Jews," he snarled, "have entered the Aryan Zone. In a big way."

"How big?" blurted Keith, never much one for protocol.

"Big enough," Gunnarsson replied. "Enough to set us back to square one—*if* we allow it. Which we have no intention of doing. The Liberty Circle and the Brotherhood of Aryan Skinheads should be able to nip this thing in the bud. Brother Benny here will explain."

A pudgy skinhead with amazingly thick glasses got to his feet. I started; I'd seen this guy before. He ran the disc shop across from Captain Nemo's. This was the head of the Brashboys? I'd heard no end of rumours. Like how he'd been made the head because the last guy had got himself murdered. How this guy's leadership wasn't as effective. How he'd apparently decided it was safer to throw himself in with the Liberty Circle. But whatever the reason, the Brashboys were part of the Circle now. That was something you had to respect.

He cleared his throat and puffed himself up like a balloon. "We've just discovered," he announced, "that the old library building across from McTavish Park was recently sold. Unfortunately, it was sold to Jews. Without our even knowing, they have been converting it into a new home for the Jewish Centre. That means they'll be publishing their local newsletter there and holding all kinds of meetings. It means a recreation centre, complete with an auditorium/gymnasium. It means a synagogue as well. All the Jewish celebrations will be celebrated there. And—it opens in four days! There'll be Jews running all over the place—including our park."

"All over our park," the shadow above us growled. *"All—over—our—god—damned—Zone!"*

The sudden fury startled all of us, and we sat stunned as its echo resonated through the room. Even Benny paled, as if certain Gunnarsson blamed him personally. But when he spoke again, Gunnarsson's voice was controlled and paced. Low, like a switchblade.

"We will not allow this. Our Leader will not allow it. By the time I deliver my third report to him on this matter—the fourth at the very most—I expect us to have the matter solved."

"We will have to work quickly," Benny put in. "Both of our forces together. We—"

"We are one force," the Gunnarsson-shadow corrected. "The Liberty Circle and Brotherhood of Aryan Skinheads are both answerable to the Leader."

"Yes. That's what I meant. We'll have to work as a unit, one for all and all for one."

Gunnarsson sighed. He turned slightly and the crimson light above him lit his face grotesquely—especially his eyes, which glistened with hate. He looked like the devil, I suppose, though I didn't see it at the time. "What can we do," he asked us, "to prevent this from happening?"

Across from me, the beefy skinhead Chet grinned maliciously. "We could plug up the vents and flood the place with poison gas."

"A fire," suggested Brother Tony. "A great big one."

"Or a lot of little ones," I said. "Make them paranoid so bad they won't have anything to do with the place."

"Swarm 'em," said another. "Just grab one or two a day and beat the living hell out of them, till they get the message and leave."

"There's biological warfare," boomed Chet. "I got a soldier magazine at home tells how to do it."

"Or," suggested Benny, "I know someone who can get us explosives."

That one set off a ripple of laughter—one that didn't reach Gunnarsson. I glanced up to see him staring at Benny intently.

"Who?" he asked.

Benny blinked. "Who?"

"Who can get us explosives?"

"My...my cousin works in a mine. He snuck some out once, just a little, just for kicks. He works with the stuff, you know, and he can get it past security if he really wants. But...what would we do with it?"

Gunnarsson was silent for a long time, staring at Benny in the red light.

At last, he said, "We will use every technique at our disposal to influence these people as much as possible. We will do what we can to make them listen to common sense. In the end, if they set up Jew Central in the middle of the Aryan Zone anyway...we will take off our white gloves. We'll do what we must. And they will leave." He leaned back on the stage, casting his face into shadow again. "Personally, I wouldn't mind something spectacular. It could be just the publicity we need."

We talked deeply into the night, puzzling out a course of action. More than once, a Brother had to poke me in the ribs to keep me alert. I'd had only four hours sleep the night before, and I'd get less than that tonight. I had to be in a mall downtown first thing in the morning, canvassing Christmas shoppers.

We finally came up with a plan, and committed it to memory. We'd had to do more and more memorizing of details these days, at a time when my brain was failing me. But Gunnarsson wanted nothing written down or stored on a disc, nothing that could incriminate us later if something went wrong. One detail was easy to remember, though.

The key player was going to be me.

Icy air blasted into my face, jolting me awake—I'd left the church with the others without even being conscious of it. The shock snapped me into full awareness, and everything took on a clarity I hadn't experienced in weeks. Had I been walking, talking and sleeping, all at the same time?

For the very first time, I realized fully that autumn was over. It was cold out, a bitter winter sort of cold. The snow squealed beneath our feet, no longer fluffy and new. The trees we passed hung heavy with frost. Here and there these were highlighted with Christmas lights.

"What...what's today's date?" I blurted.

Gunnarsson looked at me closely. "It's December Fourth. Why do you ask?"

"I was just curious, sir. I guess it's not important."

Except, for one brief moment, I'd wondered if my birthday had passed. It hadn't; I wouldn't be seventeen for another couple of months. Not that it mattered. Birthdays were ignored in the Circle. But something in me wanted to remember it, to know on the day that it happened just what day it was. As if a fraction of me had stayed behind in the old world, while the rest of me lived in the Liberty Circle.

As we neared Liberty Hall, I noticed Gunnarsson regarding me closely. At the same time, the weariness and fatigue began to return, and my brain emptied itself of everything again. Everything, that is, but the date, and how long it was to my birthday.

The thought of it filled my mind, displacing the usual chant, and the rest of the trip back didn't seem half so cold.

Eighteen

What's the matter, Kent? Cat got your tongue?"
I started.

I'd been sitting there like a lump as usual, paying no attention. "I'm sorry," I said. "What was the question?"

There were laughs from the other guys seated on the gymnasium floor. Rabbi Goldberg looked annoyed. "What question? I hadn't asked you anything. I'm just curious why you never seem to contribute anything to these discussions. What's on your mind, Kent? You act like you're somewhere else."

I shrugged, feigning ignorance as best I could. "I don't know," I said stupidly. "I guess I'm just tired or something."

The rabbi waved a hand. "There's coffee on the table. Get some, brother, and get awake already."

Brother? For an instant, that stopped me cold. Had they figured out who I was? Were these youth group discussions being staged for my benefit? Maybe that's why they never delved into the usual conspiracy lies. Not once had I heard about how Jews were the master race.

But, no—I was only being paranoid. I took the rabbi's advice and got up to get some coffee. It was important to stay alert, here in the lions' lair.

I'd been playing this game for a week and a half, since the Jewish centre had opened. I'd wandered in the very first day, armed with a bucket of lies. I was Kent, a senior, and I'd been away from the synagogue since elementary school. I was interested in coming back. Could they provide me with some information?

The rabbi had nearly tripped over himself in his rush to take me in. He had sat and talked with me for half an hour. I'd given him my whole life history—all carefully rehearsed, of course—and he'd told me about these youth drop-ins after school. Mainly they involved basketball, something I'd once been good at. After that, he'd said, there'd be "fellowship discussions". And, I thought, opportunities to snoop around.

But it was what had happened after that meeting that really clinched my role. I'd arrived late in the afternoon, so by the time the rabbi had finished with me, it was time to close up shop. We'd left the building together, parting on the steps. It was nearly dark already.

I'd started down the street, a new chant streaming through my brain. *Fifty-five days to my birthday*, it said, *fifty-five days to my birthday*... I was halfway down the block before I noticed the skinheads. There were four of them, Brashboys, and Chet was in the lead.

"Jew-boy," he growled when we were close enough to speak. "Hey, Jew-boy—you're on the wrong street."

I stopped. What the...

When they reached me, Chet gave me a shove that sent me into the gutter. For a moment, I was genuinely confused. Then I remembered Allan's warning: "We'll have to make you look like you really are a Jew. Be prepared for anything." He hadn't explained what he meant, and now it looked like he wouldn't have to. I looked up, and all four were bearing down on me.

Then I heard a piercing shout and the sound of running feet: Rabbi Goldberg was coming to the rescue. It was pretty brave, I guess, but also pretty stupid. They set into us good, only with him they weren't pretending. He was flat on his back in seconds. The skins took off down the street.

The attack had its desired effect. The rabbi seemed closer to me after that, as if he felt partly to blame. That was fine with me. I would bask in his pity for as long as he wanted—and spy on the centre every chance it gave.

The incident gave him and the other Jews second thoughts about what they were doing. I heard them discussing it on one of my subsequent visits. Apparently they'd known already about the Aryan Zone. They'd planted themselves there on purpose in order to screw up our plans. Bad move, they were beginning to find. Yet they stubbornly refused to leave.

Now, as the group broke up for the day, the rabbi took me aside. He didn't look so peeved anymore.

"I'm sorry I got on your case," he said, "but I really am concerned. You're too quiet for a guy your age. And, dude—" He looked me up and down. "You're not healthy. Not at all. I was watching you play today. It occurred to me that if you were any thinner, we could use you for a microphone stand.

"I'm not trying to be rude, Kent. You seem to know what you're doing out there, and yet half of me says you shouldn't even be playing. You came off at the end of the game panting like a racehorse." He put a hand on my shoulder, the way a caring teacher might. "Is there something you'd like to tell me? Are you...ill, maybe? Because if you don't think you are...well, I really think you should consider seeing a doctor. You seem to be suffering fatigue."

I stared at him a moment, saying nothing. I was fatigued, all right—because of people like him. People who plotted to take over the world, while those who fought them had to constantly scramble.

"I'm all right," I said at last. "It's nothing major."

He frowned, as if disappointed. He brushed a longish strand of red from his brows, a strand that was shot with grey. "If you don't want to talk about it, fine. As long as you know I'll listen. But it's something I've noticed in you, Kent—you don't let people in. When you're with the others, you hardly share anything of you. Half the time you act as if you're not entirely there. Sometimes, like today, you don't even respond to your own name."

I considered that. The rabbi, it seemed, knew something was up—he just didn't know what it was. But if he wanted to believe it was personal problems, then that's the way it would be. I'd give him what he wanted. "Well," I began, "there were a couple of things..."

He gave me his undivided attention for the better part of an hour, while I made up problems for him to solve. He bought all of it. It was hard not to feel a little guilty, though: he did seem genuinely concerned. But a chant chased that guilt away.

Finally he glanced at his watch. "I've got to lock up,"

he said. "Our receptionist will be waiting to leave."

"You want these basketballs put away?" The ones we'd been practising with were strewn about the gym.

"Nuts. Yeah, would you, Kent? When you're done, we should be ready to go. We can all leave together, and Mrs. Kropp and I will walk you to your station." He didn't have to say why.

The attack on us hadn't been the first attack in the Zone. It sure wasn't the last, either. Every day, I heard about a new incident—occasionally I even glimpsed a battle in progress. Before long, the cops started patrolling the area more. *That* was a laugh. They didn't really understand what a menace the Brashboys could be. For one thing, skinheads always dispersed when ordered to do so.

But as soon as the cops were around the corner, another Jew would get jumped. Some had started fighting back. They were getting organized. The Aryan Zone was gradually turning into a war zone.

I went around gathering all the balls I could carry, kicking the others toward the half-completed stage. When I reached it, I stopped and stared. The next phase of the Liberty Circle's plans had just clicked into place in my mind.

It was a stage like we'd had in school, with giant drawers that rolled from beneath. You could get a lot of equipment in one of those drawers. You could even hide a person.

You could even hide a bomb.

I'd been shown the device once, when it was still only partly built. The active ingredient was some explosive I'd never heard of, supposedly more stable than dynamite.

Brother Benny of the skinheads had come through well, getting us that. The bomb would be triggered by a remote control built by Brother Quinton. Carefully.

In six days' time, the stage would be complete, and the Jewish Centre would hold its grand opening. It was to be an open house, with a programme in the gym after lunch. The media had been invited, as well as local dignitaries; the room was sure to be packed. The speeches would be delivered from a lectern on the stage, probably directly over the middle drawer.

I would place the bomb in that middle drawer.

The plan was not to hurt anyone. We'd be phoning in a warning. We'd have an agent in the audience, someone who would watch to make certain the room was cleared. Then he would step onto the street with the crowd and press the magic button in his pocket.

The centre of the stage would erupt, the lectern smashing through the ceiling. Basketballs would be blown to bits. The long tables flanking the lectern would flip to either side, and water pitchers would shatter. A flash fire would result, one that might cause considerable damage. The Jewish Centre would close its doors, possibly for good. No one would want anything to do with it. Terrorism would accomplish what gentler techniques had not.

"Kent?"

I turned, and saw the rabbi with his jacket on. He looked at me inquisitively.

"Just dreaming again," I said with a smile. I bounced the basketballs into the drawer and pushed it smoothly shut.

The chant carried me home to Liberty Hall and did not allow a single incorrect thought. It kept out the image of the smile Mrs. Kropp had met me with that day. It stopped me from remembering the sincerity with which Rabbi Goldberg had listened to my "problems". It shut out what could happen if something went wrong, and someone wound up getting hurt. It kept clear for me what our goals were, what we had to do to keep the world free. It made my mind officially "pure" as I reported to Brother Allan and kept it that way until my head hit the pillow.

Then dreamless sleep took over.

I bolted upright at the touch on my shoulder, ready to break into the morning chant. A hand clapped over my mouth. The room was still dark, I realized, and silent save for the sounds of my Brothers' breathing.

"Shhhh." The whisper exploded in my ear, jarring me fully awake. I sat still, heart pounding, wondering what new test I was about to face. My accoster stayed quiet, as if fearful someone would hear. A minute or so went by before he gradually released his grip. I turned, and in the dim glow from the window, saw Benny Anderson.

"Brother Corey," he whispered. "I have to talk to you."

I knew instantly something was wrong. Talking like this at night was strictly against the rules—a fact Benny seemed to remember well. He kept glancing around as if terrified of being discovered.

"Maybe," I suggested, "you should wait until morning."

He shook his head. "No. Something's wrong, Corey. Those explosives you're supposed to carry—"

"I don't think I want to hear this."

"There's too many of them. They'll wipe the place off the map."

"Go away. Go to sleep, Brother Benny, or I'll report you."

"Corey, *listen*. Just think about it a minute. They keep us pretty busy here. So much that we haven't got time to think. Except sometimes—"

"Too much thought is a waste of time," I snapped. "You're letting Doubt get the best of you. Say the chant."

He shook his head again. "I can't. It's too much. There's something very wrong!" His voice was becoming less and less of a whisper. In the room's dim light, I thought I saw someone move.

Beneath the flimsy blanket that covered me, I could feel my heart pounding fast. Maybe this was a test. Maybe the elders had sensed my own Doubt and had sent Benny here to spy. Or was Benny really a Doubter himself? My mind was too fogged to work it out. I needed sleep.

"Go to bed, Brother," I said at last. "You'll feel better about it tomorrow." It struck me as ridiculous, speaking like that to someone older than me—the leader of the Brashboys, yet!

In the darkness, I saw him frown. "But..." he began, then seemed to reconsider. Maybe he was scared I'd actually report him. Or maybe, if he really was a spy, he thought I'd passed the test. Whatever the case, he crept away in the dark and did not return that night.

I couldn't sleep after that, despite my exhaustion. Images hurled themselves at me from the shadows, filling my mind with Doubt. What if innocent people got hurt? What if Rabbi Goldberg wasn't as evil as I'd been led to believe? I chanted in the darkness, and sweated and chanted some more, but this time the Doubts wouldn't leave. I'd have to confess them soon. And I'd have to turn Benny in.

I began to wonder how many other Doubters there were, and whether our Leader ever made mistakes. The Doubt in my mind got bigger and bigger until I thought I was coming apart.

When the first notes were strummed for our morning wake-up, I rose and hurried to find Brother Allan.

Nineteen

I found Allan in the kitchen, directing breakfast traffic. The Christmas season was in full swing, and our canvassing teams were blitzing the malls like never before. There'd been more recruitment dinners lately, too, and a lot more successful recruitments. Liberty Hall was fast becoming a crowded place.

I interrupted Allan and asked to speak with him alone. From the tone of my voice, I think, he knew right off something was wrong. He pawned his duties off on a Sister, and we went in search of an empty room.

I told him about Benny.

And I let him sense, just a little, that I was having Doubt. I didn't go into detail, though, not even when he prodded. It suddenly seemed a better idea to just let the past few hours of worry slide by. I'd screwed up once already, with the leaflet campaign. I didn't want him to think I couldn't be trusted.

"Good," Allan told me when I'd finished. "You did the right thing, Brother Corey, coming to me like this. You've protected the Circle, and more than that, you've shielded Benny from harm. We can't help doubters unless we know they're doubting. He'll be happy again,

I'll see to it. We are all sheep here, but also shepherds—we take care of one another."

He took a tiny notebook from his pocket and flipped through it. "I think I'm going to give you a change of pace today. Skip the Jewish Centre, Brother Corey. Instead...yes, I'm going to put you here, on Sister Julie's canvassing team. You haven't worked with Julie for a while, have you?"

"No," I said, trying to hide the little flutter of excitement I felt. Feelings like those I had for Julie were frowned on by the Liberty Circle. Dating was unheard of, and even marriages had to be approved by our Leader. It didn't matter, anyway. Julie was twenty-one, at least four years older than me.

When I took my place at the breakfast table, I suddenly didn't feel so hot. I was light-headed and dizzy, and the floor seemed a long way off. It was all I could do to raise a glass to my lips. Small wonder. I was averaging four hours sleep a night.

Julie came to me right after morning chores. "Oh, Brother Corey," she said, giving me a great big, predictable hug, "it's just so good to be working with you again!" She smelled of perfume, something else that wasn't allowed. But exceptions were made sometimes when we had to work in public. We wanted to make an impression, after all.

We dressed in winter parkas and jammed into a car with two other teams. I wound up crammed between a door and Sister Julie, who didn't seem to notice the closeness at all. I myself did a lot of chanting.

They let us off at a busy downtown corner, where we

went into our usual act. Today we were selling poinsettias, "to sponsor a Christmas party for needy kids". We didn't actually have the plants, of course, we were just promising their delivery.

The people we approached seemed infected with the season. Julie was cleaning up, though I wasn't doing so well myself. I couldn't seem to focus. The world kept fading out. A couple of times, I thought I might even faint.

Julie wandered over, her face showing concern. "You look tired, Corey," she said. "Are you going to be all right?"

I shrugged. "I didn't sleep too well. I wish I could beam over to Liberty Hall to get a cup of coffee." There were several pots brewing there at any given time; I wasn't the only one who stayed awake too much.

Julie frowned. "Okay, I'll tell you what. I'm going into this office building to try my luck with the poinsettias. What say you give me the money you've raised and head across to the mall? I'll meet you in the food court as soon as I make my quota. We'll get you a cup of coffee and a great big juicy burger—I know what you think of the food at Liberty Hall! Then we'll do more poinsettias."

I watched her enter the office building, my mind in a fog; I would have expected UFOs before I expected this. Numbly, I turned and started for the corner. Food, I thought, real live food. Food that wasn't boring—or particularly cheap. We weren't to waste money like that, but if Julie said okay...the light turned green, and I stepped off the curb toward a *real, live hamburger*.

And that's all I remember.

I didn't see the van that tried to beat the lights. I don't

recall its driver hitting the brakes, locking the wheels on a patch of ice. I never heard the screams of passers-by as my body flew through the air.

All I can remember is the promise of that damned hamburger.

Twenty

I emerged at last into a world of searing light. A buzzing came from the light, and I thought my head would explode with it. I screamed and screamed, or thought I did. All I heard was a pathetic moan.

"Hello, there. Are you back with us again?" Somebody touched my forehead.

I forced my eyes open against the glare. It came from a fluorescent fixture above. In its harsh light, a uniformed nurse gazed down at me.

"Now, just relax," she said, in a patronizing voice. "You've been in a little accident. You're probably in some discomfort now, but you're going to be okay."

"Accident...?" My voice was a rusty turnstile.

"You were hit by a car," she said. "You've been asleep for most of the day."

"I don't remember. Please—my head hurts..."

She went and got me some Aspirin. Sitting up for it was all I could do, but she wouldn't leave me alone after that. She whipped out a clipboard and pen. "All this time," she said, brushing a strand of grey from her head, "and we've no idea who you are! What is your name, please?"

"Kent," I replied automatically. "Kent Cohen." The

accident, it seemed, had not loosened the Circle's grip. It still dictated my answers.

"How old are you, Kent?"

"Nineteen." I'd said it before I knew why, though I realized a few seconds later. If I'd told her "sixteen", it would make me a minor, someone whose parents had to be found. I had to convince them I was no one's concern but my own. I could have told her "eighteen", of course, but somehow "nineteen" sounded less like a lie.

She scratched it in without blinking an eye. "What is your address?"

I gave her the address of Liberty Hall.

"Where do you work?"

"I don't."

"Are you a student, then?"

"Yeah. Community college."

"Who should we notify about this? Family members, friends—you must have a whole army of people worried sick about you!"

I thought about that one carefully. "I live with my cousin," I said slowly. "Allan—" I stopped, and realized with a dull horror that I'd forgotten the guy's last name! All I could remember ever calling him was "Brother Allan". And now nursy was giving me the fish-eye, waiting for that other name. Think fast, I told myself, think real fast...

"His name is Brother Allan," I said lamely.

She raised an eyebrow. "'Brother' Allan? Is he a monk?"

"Sort of. The place is called 'Liberty Hall'. It's a religious commune."

The other eyebrow went up. She scratched some more on the pad. "Are you married?"

Married? Good grief! "No," I said, and I couldn't suppress a grin. "I'm not."

"All right." She smiled back. "Just a few more questions, then..." She asked me about my family history, what allergies I had, and so on. At last, she set the clipboard aside.

"How are you feeling now? Is the pain a little better?"

"A bit," I said. "I still hurt all over, though."

"I'm not surprised. You've got a welt on your skull, bruised ribs, sprained tendons in your left arm and bumps and scrapes all over. You're lucky, though—it could have been worse."

"Is it anywhere near lunch time?" I asked hopefully.

"It's eight o'clock in the evening. But of course we'll feed you!"

She left to get me a meal, so I lay in bed and experimented with moving various parts of my body. I felt much better when I didn't do that.

I looked about the room. There was only one other bed, and it was empty.

I was the only person there.

A fluttering rose in my chest, a giddy little feeling of excitement. I couldn't remember the last time I'd been alone. For weeks now, there'd been people around me constantly. Now there was no one. There was nobody there, and I'd slept for over a day.

I could think.

We were supposed to chant when that happened. We were supposed to fill our minds with the Liberty Circle

Creed and nothing else. But I didn't. As hard as I tried to, the need for it just didn't seem to be there—and I did need to think, if only to dispel the doubts that had invaded my mind.

But the food came then, so I sat up and all but licked the plates clean.

Then, when there was nothing left to devour, I pushed the tray away and lay back in the crisp, starched sheets. Now, I thought, now I will think.

And I fell asleep again.

I dreamed, a happy dream at first. Neil and Lisa were there. We were hanging out at the mall, and everything was like before—until some weird choir started singing. And then I woke and discovered the choir was real.

"Oh, Corey, Corey, we love you so,
The world's not the world without you, you know,
We searched and searched for you,
all through the night,
We're so happy, so happy, so glad you're all right!"

I counted eight of them, though in the confined space of the hospital room, there might as well have been eighty. Allan was there, and Julie. The doorway was lined with curious nurses. The one who'd admitted me was there, and she looked sort of puzzled. I remembered telling her my name was Kent.

The other bed in the room had been filled. The guy inside it was black.

Allan came forward to shake my hand. "Brother Corey, it's just so good to see you alive and well." His idea of "alive and well", I thought, needed to be adjusted.

"Oh, Brother Corey..." Julie came round the other side of the bed, the worries of the world etched into her face. "This is all my fault. I should never have left you alone like that."

Allan nodded. "Sister Julie broke one of our Leader's directives when she did that, Brother Corey. But she is very, very sorry."

"Yes," Julie agreed, though I thought I detected a slight flatness to her voice. "I will make it up to you, Brother Corey. I will make it up to everyone. I'll take over your canvassing duties while you're here, by doubling my own."

Doubling her own? I shook my head. "You can't," I said, my voice a rasp from sleep. I could suddenly see how exhausted she looked, how dark the bags beneath her eyes were. "You don't get enough sleep, or—"

Julie put a hand over my mouth, cutting off what I wanted to say. "Let's do a chant together. It will keep your mind off your hurts."

"No," I blurted. "I want to rest for a while. I want to think."

"Too much thought," Allan reminded, "isn't good for you. Come on, Brother, we're your family. Don't you think we know what's best?" He glanced at the others, who jumped in on cue with the usual gushings of brotherly love.

So I did the chant with them, if only to get them off my case. It wasn't like before, though. This time I kept part of me back, a little piece of my mind that I refused to erase with the chant. I filled that little piece with an unofficial thought: my birthday.

Then a nurse came in and told everyone visiting hours were over. Allan hung back as long as he dared, filling my head with warnings:

"Don't talk to anyone, Brother—*especially* the coon in the next bed. Do the chant, over and over, every waking hour till we get you out. Don't drift for an instant—you're far too important to us to be brainwashed by conspirators. And don't worry about the Jewish Centre. We're sending Brother Tony there in your place." He grabbed my hand and squeezed it. "You've done well, Brother," he whispered. "Thanks to you, the Jewish Centre in the Aryan Zone will soon be a thing of the past!"

And then he was gone, seconds ahead of the nurse who'd come to throw him out.

I lay back in bed and waited for that clearness of mind to return. It didn't, not right away. The chanting and mosquito-like closeness of the past hour had muddled it up. When the future of the Free World is riding on your shoulders, there seems no room for idle thought.

But I remembered my birthday again, and that got the juices flowing. It was a day meant just for me, a tribute to my being alive. I focused on that until slowly, the fog began to lift. Gradually, I could think again.

"Those all your people here, meeting you like that?"

No. I closed my eyes tight and willed myself to ignore him. That's all I needed—the black guy trying to start a conversation. Just leave me alone, I thought. I want to think.

"Never saw anything like it," he continued, ignoring my silence. "You folks some sort of religious organization?"

I lay with my eyes closed, ignoring him.

"Oh, I see," he said, a growing edge to his voice. "The silent treatment, right? 'Don't talk to anyone—especially the coon in the next bed.' That it?"

I stayed silent.

"Your so-called 'religion', does it tell you about loving one another, about unity of the races? About how all of us are God's children? Et cetera?"

"Not everyone believes in those things," I said hotly. I turned my head in time to see the black guy's eyebrows shoot up toward his hair, which was lightly dusted metallic grey.

"You mean to say," he began, "your group *doesn't* believe in those things?"

"We don't. So what?"

"I heard your friends speak of love, of saving the world. What the hell was that about?"

"That doesn't have to mean saving it for everyone. It's a free country. We've got a right to our opinions."

"*Opinions!*" He paused for a moment, glaring at me. The little TV suspended above his bed continued to squawk the news through its tinny speaker; something about some gun shop that had got itself robbed. He reached up and flicked it off. Wincing slightly, he rolled gingerly on his side to face me. "What's the matter with you, white boy? Your mother drop you on the head as a kid? What gives you the right to act like this?"

"Because there is a conspiracy." There, it was out. I realized I was going to blab it all, about the Liberty Circle and everything, to a member of the Lower Races. I knew that immediately, but what I didn't know was why. Maybe it was an effect of the pain reliever. Maybe I thought I'd make this black person see our way of thinking. Or maybe, just maybe, it was something else entirely.

I needed to tell someone.

I needed to tell about my doubts, and not to someone from the Circle. My family was out of the picture, and so were most of my friends. But I needed *someone* to listen, and I needed it right away. And this guy, this African, this enemy of the Circle, was the only person available.

His eyes had gone wide, and he was grinning like someone who'd just encountered a moron. "All right. All right. I'm not gonna bust your chops. I'm gonna chill here, okay?" He shook his head. "Damn. I really, really want to bust your chops."

My chops were already busted—but that didn't stop me from rolling on my side to toss him the appropriate sneer. "Better not," I warned. "The Circle would be on you like ugly on an ape. Maybe they will anyway."

I swear, the guy turned a deeper shade of black right there in front of me. I thought his eyes would explode. "I think," he rumbled, "we shouldn't talk to each other. Not even a little bit."

We wound up doing exactly that, though, long into the night. We talked about everything.

Twenty-One

Late afternoon rays streamed in through the windows, touching the patients' lounge with one last coat of gold. I watched a cancer patient across the room shove another smoke into his mouth, and I sighed heavily.

"I don't understand it," I said. "I'm not stupid. So why did I believe so many lies?"

"Because you had every reason to believe they were truths." Sam Winston creaked back in the leather upholstery, his brown skin bronzed in the winter light. His eyes looked like road maps, which wasn't too surprising; we'd been at it again all day. I felt a burning shame whenever I remembered the way I'd treated him earlier. He really should have thumped me one by now. A couple of times he nearly had.

"You almost *had* to believe them," Dr. Harron put in. He lay sprawled on the couch by the windows, dishevelled as a worn-out J-cloth. "In that isolation, with virtually everyone else doing the same thing, not going along would've been difficult—even for someone with a lot more years tucked under his belt. Plus, you were being manipulated. That 'whispering' from the woods, for example—probably an attempt at subliminal persuasion. And you told me about other things that smack suspiciously of behaviour modification, like the chanting they taught you to block out thought. And the way everyone fell asleep so quickly your first night there...they may have used drugs on you.

"So when everyone else bought the story, or seemed to, you went along too. I think anyone would have. In fact..." he scratched at a day-old beard, "I know it."

I looked from one to the other, these new friends of mine, wondering how they could have seemed like enemies just days ago. It had been a long, driving, wild, crazy week. And it hadn't really picked up speed until the morning of my fourth day there.

That's when I'd risen and left our room, the first time ever since the accident. I'd winced in pain every step of the way, until the patients' lounge at the end of the hall came within reach. I'd taken the door just before it, and entered the drafty stairwell.

I couldn't use the elevator; it was by the nurse's station, and they'd be sure to see me go. By the time I'd climbed three floors, though, my ribs were ready to bust through my chest. I emerged at last at some other ward's lounge, where I collapsed in the nearest chair.

They'd come each day, the Circle, fifteen minutes before visiting hours. They hadn't left, not once, not until the nurses chased them out at night. There'd been two or more at a time, and they never let me think. I needed them out, and I needed freedom from chanting. I needed freedom from Sam, too; I'd almost seemed to get something out of our arguments at first, but less so as time went on. The night before, we'd nearly come to blows. So I'd come here, to hide and to think.

Think I did, just about up to noon. I thought about so many things.

Then a deep booming voice blasted me out of it: "Are you completely out of your mind?"

I looked up to see Sam in the doorway, furious. "Leave me alone," I pleaded.

"Your people are looking for you. You've got half the hospital turned upside down."

"I need to be alone. Can't you just leave me alone?"

He came toward me. "Look, your Ku Klux posse has started without you, and that chanting's driving me nuts. Why don't you go and keep them amused?"

"I can't do the chant! I can't!"

The sudden desperation in my voice stopped him cold. He stopped before me and stared a long while. "You really can't, can you?" he muttered, almost to himself. "It's like you don't even want them in there."

I looked up sharply. "I never said that," I told him. "Please don't tell them that. All I want is to be by myself for a while. I only want to think."

As I watched, Sam's expression slowly changed, to something like recognition. "Sonnovabitch. I just figured it all out. I can't believe I didn't before."

"Leave me alone!"

Instead, he took a seat next to me, uninvited. "This camp you told me about—where you learned about the 'conspiracy'. It was real isolated, right? Somewhere far from town?"

I looked at him suspiciously. "What if it was?"

"They kept you pretty busy there, didn't they?"

"I don't want to hear this." I turned away.

"I told you what I do for a living—all the streets I've helped pave in this city. Well, way back when I was not much more than a snot-nosed kid like yourself, we had this guy on our crew. He was a friend of mine—a *white* friend, by the way—and he got himself into some kinda weird group." Sam shook his head. "Wound up with his head shaved, selling flowers on a windy corner. Wouldn't have a thing to do with me after that, even with his own family."

"Yeah?" I looked back to him, half-curious. "So what'd you do?"

He looked at me a moment, then looked past me out the window. "Nothing. I didn't do nothin'" He got up suddenly and left the room, without another word. I stared at the empty doorway, wondering how long it would take until he sent the others my way.

I didn't know it then, of course, but he was making a few inquiries. It took a while, he told me later. He hadn't known whom to call.

Eventually, he returned with Dr. Harron. Dr. Harron, I soon found out, was more than just a physician. He was someone who'd once kidnapped his own brother, snatching him from the clutches of a cult. He'd learned a lot about cults then and had made a point of learning more. Freeing people's minds had become a full-time preoccupation.

He was a deprogrammer.

At first, when I'd realized what he was, I'd withdrawn into myself like a turtle. They were evil, I'd been warned, servants of the conspiracy who attacked the Liberty Circle every chance they got. They were, if one believed in such a thing, agents of the devil. They were the worst possible thing that could happen to me.

Hasty arrangements were made. I was taken to a different wing and shut in a room with Dr. Harron and another doctor, who turned out to be a shrink. Sam was there, too, partly at his insistence—and partly at mine. It made no sense, but I suddenly wanted him around. He may have been a member of the 'Lower Races', but I'd come to realize he was no agent of the devil. Plus, his was the only familiar face around outside of the Circle.

They talked to me, for hours on end. I didn't respond, not at first. But they persisted, and eventually I granted them a few mumbled answers just to appease them. They didn't let up, though—instead, they started telling me about the cults.

I'd never heard about cults, not about how they operated, anyway. They were organized groups, I was told, who brainwashed people into serving twisted causes or moneyed leaders. They changed you into something like a zombie. They never told you who they were, not at first, in case you'd heard of them. They disguised themselves as churches, self-improvement groups, even political parties. Often they would get you to come to a meeting, then try to convince you to go off to a camp or retreat in some isolated place. They would keep you busy after that, never a moment to think, and they would keep you exhausted and malnourished to boot.

And you would change—into whatever they wanted you to be.

They went by many names, Dr. Harron told me. And in his opinion, they were wrong. They lied to you. They robbed you of individual thought and reason. They turned you into a robot.

The next couple of days went by like that, with Sam, Harron and the shrink each taking a crack at me. After a while I started talking more and more. Arguments at first, then questions—I had so many questions. By noon the second day, I felt about ready to snap. I was trembling and crying, and then I started to laugh. I couldn't seem to stop.

That got the psychiatrist upset, but Dr. Harron wouldn't let up. He kept at me, yelling words I can't even remember, until there was nothing left of me but a whimpering pile of nerves. Then they left me for a while, all alone in that room. A nurse brought me lunch.

And then they started all over again.

I yelled at them and swore, and a couple of times even spat. I did everything but spin my head around and vomit—which might have been appropriate, now that I think about it. But by mid-afternoon, it was all over. There weren't any reasons left to go on believing in the Liberty Circle. Every single one of them had been shot down.

My tears dried up and I started to shake again, this time out of anger. They'd lied to me—Gunnarsson and Allan and even Julie—all that stuff about how much they cared for me was nothing, nothing at all. They didn't give a damn about me.

And there was no "Master Race".

It wasn't easy, letting go of those lies. It wasn't quick. A lot of times, I felt like killing myself. And now, in the patients' lounge in the lowering light, I felt completely drained. Like nothing was left inside.

Dr. Harron rose from the couch. He gripped my hands for a moment, to stop them trembling so much.

"Enough. I think you've had enough for today. And so have you, Sam. And so have I." He stared at me thoughtfully. "How old are you, Corey? I mean, really?"

I started. What the hell—had he guessed? I'd told him the truth about my name, the truth about my family—though I'd never said who they were—the truth about absolutely everything but my age. And now he wanted that. Instead, I countered with, "What made you ask that?"

"You just don't look nineteen. My guess is seventeen, maybe younger."

"I'm eighteen."

"Oh?" He looked straight into my eyes. "You sure about that?"

"I'm eighteen," I repeated. "They told me to say nineteen. I don't know why." I flushed slightly, realizing I was replacing one lie with another. There'd been too many lies already, but there'd have to be one more. If I told them I was only sixteen, they'd ship me back to my parents the second I was released. I didn't want that to happen, ever.

Dr. Harron gazed a moment longer, then cracked a grin. "All right. I believe you. Now let's get you to bed before you drop." He slapped a hand lightly across my back and led Sam and me into the corridor. "I'm not with this hospital," he said, "but I'll see if I can get you moved to this wing. Hopefully that'll throw off your admirers, until we can get rid of them for good. But I'd like you to have some company. How's about we transfer Sammy, here, too?"

"That is," added Sam dryly, "if you don't mind sharing a room with a member of the 'Lower Races'."

I looked at him and tried to apologize for everything again. Sam just grinned it off and reached to muss my hair. How lucky I was, I thought: I'd gone from a world where all the friends were fake to another, where I'd found the genuine article right off the top.

They got me to my room, where I eased carefully into bed. My body was aching, but my head was full of dreams. Life was about to begin for me—*somehow*. *Somehow* I'd get a job, my own apartment, a world of my own. I'd work during the day and paint by night, and when I'd saved enough, I'd go to college and study art. I'd move far away from the Flats, into some other part of town where artists hung out. I'd be everything I was capable of being. And no one, no one on this earth, would ever hold me down again.

The police came.

They came, just like I knew they would, and they questioned me more than I imagined they possibly could. It took three hours. Was I certain about the plot against the Jewish Centre? How many people were involved? Names? At what point did I begin to believe in the conspiracy? Why didn't I resist when asked to smash Yannick's window? Why didn't I resist when I learned about the plot against the Jewish Centre? Why didn't I resist when...

They even asked if I knew anything about the gun store that had been robbed—as if *that* had to do with anything! Dr. Harron was there for much of it, and he defended me every step of the way. The more accusatory their questions became, the more agitated he got. The police eventually threw him out. Sam got himself excused the same way a few minutes later.

At last, mercifully, they left. By this time I was exhausted, but sleep took its time in coming. How long, I wondered, would it take the Liberty Circle to crumble? How many people would be arrested? How many would get away? And how many, in the end, could really be blamed for their actions?

Was I one of them?

I started awake. I'd been having a dream, a warm, happy one that I should not have awakened from. I lay motionless for a moment, hanging onto the afterglow as long as I could.

It was dark—the curtains round my bed were drawn, and the night-light in the room was out. That was odd. I'd imagined nurses liked to strut down the halls and check on all their patients by peering in through the doors. I listened and decided it was definitely late at night. Even the paging system in the corridor seemed quieter.

And then I heard something else: a rustling sound, very near. The hairs on my neck stood on end. This wasn't right.

"Sam?"

A hand came from the darkness and clamped itself over my mouth. "Don't move," its owner whispered. "It's me."

I tensed, my heart banging against my ribs. I squinted to see who it was. A shock of blond bobbed in the dark. Keith? No, Allan. No...

Gunnarsson.

He laughed, quietly, that dangerous sort of laugh that filters sometimes from unlit alleys. "Hello, Corey. We've got ourselves into a bit of a fix, haven't we?"

I fumbled for something to say, something that could ward off whatever he'd set his mind to do. Nothing came.

He sat on the edge of my bed, studying me closely. "I thought it was you in the next bed...but I got a rude shock. Life is unfair, isn't it, Corey? You get hit by a truck while canvassing for the Circle, and you wind up next to a Christly nigger. Ah, well." He glanced about furtively for a moment, listening. When he spoke again, his voice was angry and low.

"Benny Anderson is missing. The esteemed High Commander of the Brotherhood of Aryan Skinheads, gone without a trace. I do not suspect foul play. I do not suspect anything but that he's buggered off somewhere with the intent of destroying our operations. You see, there've been some problems, to put it mildly. We've got cops investigating the Liberty Circle from one end to the other." He leaned forward and peered at me closely.

"Brother Allan tells me Benny spoke to you the other day, just before he vanished. That he told you all of his little problems. So do you know where Benny is now? Do you even have an idea? And do you know what caused him to turn against us?"

I shook my head, again and again, like a frightened little kid. "No, sir," I said. "I don't."

"I'm assuming he alone is behind all this, but I have to be sure. I have to be sure. There's too damned much at stake here. Our Leader himself could be at risk!" He glared at me suspiciously. "Why have they moved you? Why aren't they letting in visitors? You haven't been brainwashed, have you? You haven't rejected the Liberty Circle..."

"No, sir!"

"Then why—"

"The police were here," I blurted.

Gunnarsson tensed visibly. "What did they want? What did you say?"

"Just what we're supposed to. That the Liberty Circle is a church, meant for everyone. That none of our members are racists. That we don't believe in violence. I didn't tell them anything, sir, except what we were told to."

He stared at me in the gloom, and I wondered if the light was strong enough to let him see the fear on my face. He just kept staring like that, for the longest time, saying nothing at all.

And then his expression changed. Something lit in his eyes, and he was looking at me with that reverence I'd seen so often in him before—as if he was looking at something terrible, but holy.

"It was you," he said softly. "Or maybe you and Benny, but definitely it was you. Wasn't it, Corey?"

And I knew what he wanted to do.

And I saw, for the first time ever, how simply capable he was of doing it. All that stopped him was the presence of Sam in the other bed. Even if Gunnarsson made a move to choke me, I'd still have time for a single shout. And he knew it. And that knowledge was all that was keeping me alive.

We stayed in this impasse for a full five seconds, ten, an eternity. Then he got up, slowly, and backed away to the door. He didn't say a thing. The hardness in his eyes said it all.

It was a long time after he left before I dared to reach for the call button by my bed.

Twenty-Two

For three days after Gunnarsson's visit, I was treated like a terrorist target.

I had my own security guard. He stood outside in the hall and checked the identity of everyone who entered. Except for nurses and Dr. Harron, that left only friends of Sam's—no one came to see me but cops. At least until the second day.

That's when the reporters got hold of the story. Some genius at one of the papers found out what and who and why, and they came down on me like locusts. Well, two of them, anyway. One to ask a lot of questions, and the other to take pictures. I didn't feel like answering the questions—I didn't even have all the answers yet—and they only got a picture or two before Dr. Harron entered the room. He made them leave.

And then, on the evening of that same day, I had a visitor I'd been expecting. I cringed when he walked into the room. I didn't know what to say.

Rabbi Goldberg smiled weakly and took a seat by my bed. "Hello, 'Kent'," he said, and fell silent.

I didn't say anything either, and the silence grew and grew. It was like that time in the principal's office, just before I got expelled. It was up to me to speak.

And then a funny thing happened: the silence became too much. The self-pity started to fade, and anger took its place. The plot against the Jewish Centre wasn't my fault. It couldn't be all, entirely, my fault alone. I looked the Rabbi straight in the eye.

"If you want to hate me, fine! I can't stop you. But I can't change anything now. All I can do is tell the truth, and that's exactly what I've done!"

Rabbi Goldberg shook his head and gave a long, heavy sigh. "I don't hate you, Kent. *Corey*, I mean. I only hate your actions. You're not the first to listen to the words of a madman, if this really is what's happened."

I propped myself up on one elbow. "*If*? *If* this is what's happened?"

He held up his hands. "We gotta be sure. We gotta be sure the things you claim are not just...well, something they want you to believe, for example."

"I didn't imagine it!"

"No one said that you did."

"I told the cops everything. If you don't believe me, talk to them."

"I already have. And they are investigating your claims, believe me. Who do you think has been driving them on to do exactly that? That's why I haven't been in earlier. I've been working with the police, helping with the investigation." He pointed a finger at me. "The investigation you began."

I considered that. Maybe, I thought, it was only natural he should want to question me himself. If I were him, I'd probably want to talk to me too. Besides, he wasn't likely to grill me like those cops had. And, anyway, I owed him.

So I let him ask his questions, and it turned out not so bad. The conversation was almost friendly, in fact. Almost. And in that atmosphere I recalled a couple of things I'd somehow missed with the cops. The fact that Tony had been chosen to replace me at the Jewish Centre, for example. By the time we were done, we were both feeling a whole lot better about everything. He even invited me to the centre again, for basketball or just for talk.

When he left, I lay back in the starched, stiff sheets and watched a fly washing its hands on the ceiling. It seemed to be watching me, its magnificent eyes gleaming. "Pretty soon," I told it, "it's gonna all be over. They'll lock 'em all up and I'll be able to leave here safe—" I broke off, perplexed all of a sudden. Lock up who, I wondered?

Gunnarsson definitely. The "Leader", hopefully. Allan. And Benny. Julie? What about guys like Keith and Tony? Should all the Brashboys be nailed? What about new recruits? They'd been brainwashed, after all—or would that be an excuse? And if not, if all of them were guilty, what made me so innocent? Where did you draw the line, anyway?

Maybe we'd *all* go to jail. Or maybe it would go the other way, and Gunnarsson would get off easy. Who was to say he hadn't been brainwashed too? I shook my head.

That would take a judge to figure out.

Early in the afternoon of the third day, everything started to come apart.

Sam was laughing at some joke I'd made—I'd just rediscovered humour—when Dr. Harron marched in. He wore an expression I hadn't seen before, one that didn't include a smile.

"Corey," he said, "come with me." And the tone of his voice said now.

I followed him into the hall, where the security guard still loafed. Dr. Harron told him to take a break, then led me into an office. He didn't invite me to sit. I got the idea this wouldn't take long.

He leaned against the wall and studied me intently. "You," he told me sternly, "have not been completely honest. I thought we had an understanding."

My stomach did a slow roll. I didn't know what he was talking about, but he seemed to be onto something. I hoped it wouldn't screw things up.

He produced a folded newspaper, turned to the city page. "You made the news this morning. Congratulations. They make you look like a real hero."

I stared at the article in the middle of the page, two columns wide. YOUTH EXPOSES PLOT AGAINST JEWISH CENTRE read the headline. And below that: ...*tells of Nazi cult.* I was pictured there in my hospital bed, battered face and all.

I started to read, but Dr. Harron snatched it away.

"Half an hour ago," he said, "I took a call from Marty Copeland."

Marty! "What—what did he tell you?" I stammered.

"Among other things, that you are only sixteen."

I turned away and looked down at my feet. Marty, you bastard! "It's the only lie I told you."

"Is it? How do I know that?"

"I just didn't want to go back."

"Why not?"

"Because." I'd told him a little about my parents, but not specifically about my dad. About his temper, for example. I didn't want to tell him. I didn't want to tell anyone. There was nothing anyone could do about it that wouldn't just make things worse.

Dr. Harron opened the door. "Get back to your room, Corey. And prepare yourself for a visit from your brother."

"I—"

He made an impatient gesture. "Just go, Corey, all right?"

The whole scene came unglued completely round about supper time.

The police came. They were there every day, of course, but this time they came with an attitude. Dr. Harron came in with them, and he wasn't smiling at all.

A Sergeant Bell lowered himself into a chair while his partner went out for coffee. He drew a long, hissing sigh, and I knew this wouldn't be good. "We've done a lot of investigations, Corey, these past few days. We investigated the places you mentioned, and we investigated the people."

I leaned forward on the edge of my bed. What I needed now was good news, something to prove to the doctor that I wasn't a chronic liar. "Was I right? Did you find what I said you would?"

He sighed again and glanced at Dr. Harron. "We found a lot of things, Corey, that you mentioned the other day. We worked with the police at Liberty Lake, who checked on the camp up there."

"And?"

"We found little if any evidence of a 'cult', or Nazis, or racism. As far as the camp is concerned, all the buildings are exactly as you describe them—but that's where the similarity ends. There's a few people up there now, but all they're doing is cross-country skiing and riding horses. It's a Christmas camp for underprivileged inner-city kids. A few of them are black."

A surreal, nightmare feeling flooded into my mind. "That can't be. They must have found out before you got there..."

"We checked all through Captain Nemo's, and Mr. Gunnarsson gave us complete co-operation. The storeroom you described as being full of Nazi paraphernalia had nothing in it but an old pinball machine and business forms. All of it very, very dusty. That fellow Ranji didn't seem to know too much. And beyond a few Bibles and some incense sticks, we found nothing at all at that place called Liberty Hall."

"But that church they bought—"

"Has just been sold to someone else. And, Corey—" He glanced up again at Dr. Harron. "We have witnesses—good, reliable ones, some pretty upstanding citizens—who place Mr. Gunnarsson at a nightclub precisely when you said he was here."

"No. No. They're lying."

"This is not going to be an easy thing for you to hear.

But I think you and Dr. Harron need to have a chat, and see if you can't work this thing out. I've talked to a lot of people, and most of them don't think you're a bad person, not by any means. All they've told us, really, is that you sometimes act a little...well, a little strange."

I tensed. "What do you mean, 'strange'?"

He swallowed, loud enough for me to hear. "They say you would occasionally stay up all night at Liberty Hall, staring at the wall and chanting. They say—"

"We all did that!"

"They say you would sometimes curl up in a corner and hum to yourself for hours on end. That you would refuse food for days."

"We all—"

"They claim you once jumped out a window, in the middle of the night, and had to be rescued from subzero temperatures. That you were stark naked at the time..."

"*What?* Jesus Christ!"

"And other things, Corey, such as a tendency to hallucinate and to talk to inanimate objects. We heard a lot of people telling us a lot of things, and many of their stories matched. What I am suggesting to you, Corey, is that you and I and Dr. Harron here try to work things out together. I don't believe you are a bad person. I just think you need a little help."

Dr. Harron cleared his throat. He spoke without looking at me once. "Dr. Amstrud could help you, too, Corey. She's the psychiatrist who was with us when we...deprogrammed you."

Sergeant Bell held up a hand. "I don't doubt that some sort of mind thing may be involved here. I've come across cults before. But maybe your mind made up a few things in a subconscious attempt to persuade you to leave. There's people here who can help you with that."

I shook my head. "They're setting me up. Can't you see that? I'm not a weirdo, Sergeant. I'm not—and they're all lying."

"All right," he said quietly. He got to his feet and turned to Dr. Harron. "I'll be in touch tomorrow—just a few things to tidy up."

They started for the door together, discussing my "case" as if I weren't even there. I sat on my bed with a sense of doom sweeping through me in waves. For the first time, I saw clearly that the Circle would win. I saw exactly how they would do it.

I sat there for a long time after they left, and I guess I had myself a little cry. It was too much. It'd been that close to being over, and now it never would be.

I jumped when Sam touched my shoulder; I'd forgotten he was even there. He smiled at me, a smile like you give to a bawling little kid that's been rightly scolded for screwing up.

"Chill," he told me. "The world's full of all kinds of evil. It's people like you and me who have to bear the brunt of it." He patted me on the back. "I'm out of here tomorrow—doc says my hernia's on the mend. You just concentrate on getting there yourself. All right?"

I nodded and smiled my thanks at him, all the time knowing I'd lost him, too.

Supper came and went, but I didn't feel like eating. They took away the guard outside the door. Visiting hours passed, at least, with nothing out of the ordinary.

Marty never showed—I could just imagine why—but somehow that made it worse. As if I *wanted* him there.

That night, as the hospital slept and moaned around me, I lay wide awake in bed. Sam was visiting in the patients' lounge—once again I was by myself. Nothing but the endless chatter of the paging system, and that sickening hospital smell. And something else. A rhythmic sound from the corridor: *tap...tap...tap...*

I tensed and felt the blood speed up in my veins. Then an old woman shuffled into view through the half-open door. Her cane was making the noise. I breathed a sigh of relief and settled back in the bed. A wave of self-pity washed over me.

There was no use, no use at all left in my life. I'd be sent right back to my family. Back to hell. And there was no guarantee the Circle still wouldn't try to get to me, even if they knew they'd totally discredited me. There was the matter of revenge, of setting an example for others with "Doubt".

If I stayed.

I rose and went to the closet.

Minutes later I was in the empty corridor, moving away from the nurse's station. There was an entrance to a staircase here, beside the visiting lounge. The door swung open silently, then hissed slowly shut behind me. It banged when it closed completely, but that didn't matter now; I soon found myself on the street, headed into a December night.

Twenty-Three

The streets around me were growing familiar. Like a bat toward the dark, I was being drawn back to the Flats.

It was someplace I knew, at least. I wouldn't have to go right home. There was a laundry room in our building where I could shack out for the night. In the morning, with any luck, I would somehow catch Marty's attention. I'd get him to fetch my box of cash.

By the time I entered the abandoned lot behind our building, my feet were stinging with cold. I stopped and looked up at our suite. All the lights were on, in every room I could see. Mom and Dad usually sacked out by ten. For an instant, I wondered if they'd moved, and the thought nearly made me laugh: it was the old joke about the parents moving away while the kid was out. But then I glanced at the parking lot and spotted Dad's car. Somebody was just getting in.

Marty!

I broke into a run. Maybe for once he'd be sober. Maybe he would listen to my story, and nod, and tell me just the correct thing to do. Maybe he'd act like my older brother for once.

He looked up and saw me coming, and my hopes fell at once. The grin was that of a guy who'd "had a coupla Blues".

"Corey!" he exclaimed. "Little brother! What the hell ya doin' here?" Then, "Jesus, look at you. What're you doing out of the hospital?"

I shook my head; it would take an hour to explain that. "They said you were coming to see me."

He looked away. "Something came up."

"Where are you going?"

"Know when I get there, kid. The States, maybe. Clearin' outta here, though, that's for sure."

"What happened? Did you have a fight with Dad? With Mom?"

He laughed, a long, hard laugh. "Dad took a bus to the tar sands. He's out there looking for work. As for Mom, she's fighting with herself, man. She's in there now, swearing at invisible foes. She's been drinkin' hard for a week."

I felt as if he'd hit me. No, not this again. She'd been doing so well for so long. And not now, please, not now!

Marty got into the car and started it. I reached through the door and grabbed his arm. "What the hell do you think you're doing?"

"Borrowin' Dad's car," he replied. "Like I said, he's gone away. If he's wise, he won't be back." He paused for a moment, and as I watched, something in his eyes changed completely. "Cor? Come with me?"

That stopped me cold. Right out of the blue—it was always like that with Marty. What's more, it was tempting, real tempting. I'd already made my decision to leave. Here was transportation.

"If you come," Marty said, "I'll show you every bar and nightclub from Victoria to St. John's. I'd get you into them. And mountains, Corey, you've always wanted to see those. Sometimes I fish or go camping. Come with me and you'll meet women, all that you can handle. Some of the gals I know have sisters."

"What happened to Valerie?"

He tried to laugh again, but it came out as more of a choke. "Valerie left last week."

"How come? You mean for good?"

He shrugged. "'Spose. Maybe not. She got pissed at me for drinkin'. We had a bit of a row. I think that's what got Mom started. Oh, well..." He ran his fingers absently over the steering wheel, seeing nothing, I'm sure, but Valerie. I found myself actually trying not to feel sorry for him.

An odd thing happened then. Marty's expression changed, tightening here and loosening there until there was no doubt what he'd do next. He put his hands to his face and cried.

I nearly freaked. I'd never seen him do that before, not past the year I was six. I tried to think of something to say, but nothing intelligent came. I just stood there silently, waiting for him to finish. Real caring of me, huh?

It didn't matter to Marty. The tears were gone in a moment, and he was wiping his face with his sleeve. That silly grin returned, but for a moment I had to wonder: did this happen to him every time he lost a girl?

"Sorry," Marty said, obviously embarrassed. "Guess she kind of got to me, that one. It's okay for you, I guess. I know you weren't crazy about her."

"She was okay," I lied. "Attractive, that's for sure."

"Yeah. Yeah, she was." And he didn't sound horny and immature when he said that. Not like himself at all.

He reached out of the car and gripped my arm. "About those women we could get you," he said. "They don't have to be the kind you've seen me with. We could get you an artsy type. And I could help you, Corey, if you wanted to settle down. We could get you a place of your own, just you and the little lady. That way," he added with a grin, "I'd have a place to crash whenever I was in that town. Whatever town you chose."

I kept my mouth shut and listened as he rattled on. He offered me everything I didn't have, everything I'd always wanted. I could skip around the country for a couple of years, then do like he said and settle down. Get a nice girl, a decent job, be someone at last. Maybe I'd even change my name, to throw the Liberty Circle forever off my track.

"You don't have to deal with those Nazis, man." It was like he was reading my thoughts. "You can kiss it goodbye, you know? Come on, Cor! Come with me!"

I added up what I'd have if I stayed, and came up with a negative sum.

But then I looked at Marty, really looked at him for the first time that night. The way he sat there grinning, not a care in the world. The way he just moved on whenever troubles found him. And troubles always found him, wherever he went.

I thought about Mom, the way she was now.

"Well?" Marty asked, impatient for the road. "What do you think?"

"I think," I said slowly, "that if you are going anywhere at all, you'd better go straight to hell."

That made him jump, literally jump. The look in his eyes changed again, and I saw something I'd never seen there before. "Screw you," he muttered, "you little bastard. I've had it with you. You're nothin' but a snot-faced kid." He started the engine.

"And you," I yelled after him as he backed the car from the lot, "are an irresponsible coward!"

Marty hit the brakes, locking the wheels on ice. The car slid over the polished surface and stopped on a patch of snow. He got out and stormed toward me. I didn't move, not until he hit me with a force that sent me flying.

"You're not my brother," he snarled. Then he said something even ruder, something you'd never say to a brother. He got back into Dad's car, slammed it into gear and roared off with a spray of powder.

For the longest time after he left, I made no attempt to rise from the snow. There seemed to be no point, even as my body grew colder. Eventually, though, I thought of Mom. Would she be okay tonight? That was one little thing I could focus on, I decided. One little thing I could do to justify my existence.

I rose from the snow and walked stiffly into our building. I climbed the stairs slowly, vividly aware of my bruised ribs and other assorted hurts. Add to that a welt on my face, where Marty had struck me.

Our door was open, though no sound came from inside. I entered an apartment littered with empty bottles and cans. Mom lay passed out on the couch. She breathed so slowly I couldn't hear it, but when I touched her arm, her eyes flickered open.

"Change your mind, you little jerk?" she snapped, and she broke into a string of language that would've made a trucker blush. I pulled away in shock.

A second later, she fell silent, and a look of recognition entered her eyes. "Corey," she whispered, and those eyes filled with tears. "Oh, baby, where have you been?" And she started to cry, big, suffering sobs that made me want to join right in. Only I didn't. I'd done enough of that already.

So I just held her for a while and let her bawl herself out, until she began to get a hold of herself again. All the time she kept telling me how much she'd missed me, and how Marty had never really been her favourite, and how she'd always treated him better because Dad had seemed to want it. Maybe she meant what she said. I don't know. It didn't matter now.

She passed out again, and I pulled away to take a look around. Ever been to a party house? That's a place that's been rented to someone not so responsible, or maybe loaned while the owner's away. The rent gets paid somehow, maybe even the power and gas. But there's a party there every night. Things start to break or disappear, and the place gets flooded with pizza boxes and empties. The cops make it a regular stopping place, and eventually the owner finds out. Then all hell breaks loose and there aren't any more parties there.

Our apartment that night resembled a party house in its final stages. There was even a bit of plaster still lying in the hall—beneath a Yours Truly-sized hole in the wall.

I surveyed it all with little emotion. Our family was

trashed; it had been for a very long time. Yet something inside me still wanted to make a difference. Maybe I sensed I'd never be there again, and I wanted to do something nice.

I began by gathering every piece of trash in the house—all the empties, overflowing ashtrays, everything—and hauling it out to the dumpster. Then I got hold of a broom and shovelled up some more. I even put Mom's old vacuum together and passed that around a bit. Mom hardly even stirred. I ignored the bedrooms, especially mine; Marty and Valerie had probably been shacked up in it since I left. But I did go into the bathroom, where I damn near passed right out.

There was two month's worth of filth in there, most notably a crust of splattered puke round the can. The stench was unreal. For a moment, I considered leaving that room, too. But then I decided that if I really wanted to make a difference, this was the room to do it in.

I'm not exactly the prissy-clean type—I've been called a slob on more than one occasion. But by the time I'd finished in there, the place looked like Mr. Clean had camped in it for a week. The old lady would freak when she saw it. And with what I was about to do next, I'd see to it she got a nice, clear look.

I went around that apartment and collected every single container that still held a drop of booze—let me tell you, there were a lot. I took them all to the sink, and you can pretty much guess where it all went from there. Then I got hungry and decided to check out the fridge.

There was ketchup in there and half a bottle of mustard, and a few more cans of beer. And two mouldy oranges, and something that might once have been an onion. And that was pretty much it. I got the same story from the cupboards, where I discovered vodka and rye. I dumped the booze—I'd tossed about seventy bucks worth already—and headed into my room.

As I suspected, the place was a cesspool. I ignored it and opened the closet. If that little box was missing...

I felt it, close to the edge of the shelf. Too close. I brought it down and opened it, and my body started to shake.

My fingers thumbed through the bills: twenty ...thirty...fifty. Fifty dollars—same as the booze I'd dumped. Fifty dollars, all that was left of the nearly five hundred I'd saved.

"Son of a bitch!" I yelled, smashing the box into the wall. "SON OF A BITCH!" I whirled, landed on my bed, pounded with my fist at nothing in particular. All that money, gone. All that work earning it, all for nothing, all gone, all gone...

I forced myself to stop. All right. I clenched my teeth. All right. Fifty dollars. It's better than none. It's even better than forty. I got up, still trembling. Fine. It wouldn't stop what I was going to do. I stepped out into the hall.

I put on my jacket—my very own, not that Liberty Circle hand-me-down—and left our apartment door slightly ajar. I didn't have my key, and God only knew where it was. So I trusted Mom's security to the stars and walked five blocks to an all-night convenience store.

Where I blew most of my fifty on groceries.

I got back and locked up, full of the sensation that for

once I was doing the right thing. As soon as I'd put the stuff away, I settled in for a bite myself. I had a pizza and a burrito, washed down with a jumbo Pepsi. Not so nutritious, maybe, but it had been a million years.

When I'd finished, I cleaned out the coffee maker and set it to brew just before noon. Then I found Mom's alarm clock and set that to go off at twelve. I put it right beside her.

Next came the hard part. I got hold of a paper and pen and sat down to write a note.

> *Dear Mom:*
> *I love you. Please don't worry about me. I'll be fine.*
> *Please stop drinking. There is a light at the end of every tunnel.*
> *I will write you when I can. Please don't worry.*
> *   —Corey.*
> *P.S. There is food in the fridge and a bit more in the cupboard. You need to get your strength up.*

I thought about adding something about having a Merry Christmas, then thought better. I looked lamely at what I'd written. *A light at the end of every tunnel*—Jesus! But it was the best I could manage right then. I set the note by the alarm clock, got my jacket back on, and gave Mom a kiss on the cheek. As an afterthought, I got some blankets to cover her up. She didn't even stir—and wouldn't, I knew, until noon.

Then I left our place, locking tightly behind me the door to which I had no key.

I entered the street at a quarter to six, with absolutely nowhere to go. It had clouded over again, and a light snow was starting to fall. The city was just beginning to stir. I reached into my pockets and pulled out the cash my little shopping excursion had left me. Eleven dollars and sixty-two cents—yeah, that would get me far. Then I realized I wouldn't go anywhere, even if I could. And it was more than just a desire not to be Marty.

If I ran—if I let the Liberty Circle chase me away—it would be because I had no control. Even if my life worked out okay after that, it still wouldn't be enough. There would always be that one small part of me that was controlled by someone else. I'd be wherever I was because of them, not because of me.

And that would never do.

If I was going to stay, though, I'd have to prove I wasn't nuts—and there was only one person around who could help. Okay, so he hadn't talked to the cops, but that was because he was scared. And he didn't know what it meant to me. I was certain if he knew I needed his help, Ranji would tell the cops everything.

I started for Captain Nemo's.

Twenty-Four

I stood in the alley behind the arcade, gazing anxiously up at the sky. Heavy snow clouds swirled above, untouched yet by morning light. But even the winter sun could not stay down much longer. And darkness was what I needed, as long as I hung around there.

The problem was, I didn't know where to find Ranji. There was a glow in the curtains of his suite—maybe he was up there having breakfast with his wife. But there was a light downstairs, too, in the window of Gunnarsson's office. Maybe Ranji had gone down early, to feed the fish or something. Or maybe the Liberty Circle, having thrown off the cops, had decided to move back in. I couldn't risk finding out.

The logical thing to do was to start with Ranji's suite. Except...I thought I could hear his voice—and it was coming from downstairs. I strained to hear, but there were snow removers working in the street beyond. Then a factory whistle blew, and a bus went by, and a siren started up.

I clenched my fists in frustration; I'd have to get closer to hear. I stepped out from behind a disposal bin, feeling nakedly vulnerable. Suddenly I could hear the voices plainly—they were getting louder fast!

I dove back behind the dumpster, just as the service door to Nemo's opened. Ranji came out, or rather was pushed, sputtering language I'd never heard him use before. Six or seven Brothers followed, most of them skins. Chet was there. I recalled with a shiver how he'd wasted me and the Rabbi in that "attack" by the Jewish Centre. He'd only been acting with me then, and he'd flattened me just the same. From the way he was glaring at Ranji, I knew he wasn't pretending now.

"You sonnova bitch," he snarled, and the menace in his voice chilled me further. "Who the hell do you think you are? Come back here! You don't freakin' shove me and get away with it!"

"I did not shove you," Ranji tossed back. "Go and screw yourself."

Hearing Ranji talk like that was like seeing Santa Claus do drugs. Whatever had happened in there, it had to be pretty severe. But it was what could happen next that scared the hell out of me.

I remember it clearly, every second of it, as if I've memorized the frames of a film. I can't forget those pictures no matter how hard I try. My friend got halfway up the stairs before Chet got hold of his ankle. Ranji kicked at him savagely, his eyes lit with terror. He must have known now he was marked for sure.

He made it to the door, but his wife had locked it tight. She never even got a chance to open it. Four skins jumped him at once, and he went down like a kitten beneath a pile of pitbulls. Whatever they wanted to do to him, there was nothing stopping them now.

And that's when I lost my mind.

I'd shot out from behind the bin and was halfway to the stairs before anyone even noticed. Chet saw me coming first. He grinned evilly and rose from the mass of bodies. "Well, looky here. They do stick together, don't they, boys?"

"*Leave him the hell alone!*" I screamed, and I started up the stairs.

Chet gave Ranji one last kick. "Fine," he said. "We'll do you first."

If I'd just stayed behind the bin, it might have been okay. They would have done what they wanted with Ranji, and maybe it wouldn't have been too bad. Maybe. But I'd gone and jumped in instead and made them switch their attention to me. I couldn't have guessed the way it would end.

The first blow hit me like a rocket, with the second not far behind. I teetered back against the railing, the old wood cracking dangerously. Then the third blow came, and when my vision cleared, I was down on my hands and knees. That's when I saw it from the corner of my eye: Ranji, bloodied but conscious, rising to my aid. No...

"Damn you, paki!" Chet grabbed him by the collar and picked him up like a broken mannequin. "I've freakin' had enough of you, mister!" He swung him completely around, once, twice...and let go.

I caught Ranji before he hit the railing, but the momentum was too much to absorb. We hit the rail together, and there was the slightest hesitation. Then we were falling, falling, and I had to let him go.

A pile of shovelled snow received me, smashing apart

like a pumpkin. The night exploded into colours I'd never seen before and stayed like that for the longest time. I couldn't breathe, couldn't even try. Maybe, I thought, I'm dead.

But the colours cleared away, and I became aware of myself again. Slowly, carefully, I sat up in the snow. My ribs felt bad, worse than they had in days. I looked about for Ranji.

He lay beside me in the cold, gazing up at the fragmented railing. He couldn't see it, though. He couldn't see anything. His head had struck a dumpster in the fall, and his brain, his consciousness, everything he ever was, had spilled out into the cold. As if to emphasize the point, a cloud of steam rose from it all into the city sky. Amazing, I thought dully, amazing how it does that. I turned over and heaved in the snow.

When I could finally lift my head, Keith Whynter was standing there flanked by a couple of Brothers. They were staring at me in triumph.

"It was you," Keith said, his voice quavering ever so little. "You did it, Corey. *You killed Ranji.*"

Twenty-Five

I looked from one face to another, each skinhead Brother in turn. It wasn't hard to see they all intended on going along with Keith's version of events—some of them, in fact, looked like they already believed it. It had been an automatic agreement, without a word being passed.

I scrambled to my feet and ran.

I don't know why they let me go. Maybe they thought it would make me look guiltier. Maybe they needed time to get their story straight. Or maybe, like me, they were stunned by the sight of a death. They had to know they'd gone too far this time.

Adrenaline took me far, across lit streets and through darkness again, until I was out of the Aryan Zone. The hurts from my accident caught up with me then, and a stitch developed in my side. I stopped on a corner and doubled over, icy air blasting through my lungs. No—this was more than a stitch from running. I'd hurt myself again, maybe seriously.

And Ranji was dead. The thought swept through me like a cold, cold wave, and a tear slipped down my cheek. He'd come to this country to better himself, to take control of his life. Like me, that control was all he'd ever wanted—and now we'd robbed him of the chance forever.

A numbing blackness flooded my mind, an anger I could scarcely control. More clearly than ever I saw the path all this would take. The Circle had played its cards right, and the Circle was going to win. I was going to spend years in prison for a crime I'd never committed.

I was starting to collect strange looks. All around me, happy, normal people were starting another day—and I was in their way, a street person, a nuisance. I could hardly go back to the hospital, though, any more than I could go back home.

Once again, I thought of running.

And once again, I wasn't that smart.

There had to be a solution, I felt, something the cops had missed. If I could prove some of what went on in the Circle, it would give me credibility. All I needed was evidence—and that evidence had to be somewhere. Gunnarsson wouldn't shut things down completely. The Leader would not allow it.

There were a couple of skinheads down the street, loitering on the walk. Brashboys? I was too far away to see, but I rounded a corner just the same. Being captured by the cops would be bad enough. Yet that would be preferable to being caught by the Liberty Circle. The Circle probably wouldn't be that nice. Probably, a trial, with all its questions and cross-examinations, would be more than it was willing to risk.

In spite of that, I was going back again. Maybe I *was* nuts.

I took my time, just to be safe. I took all day, in fact. By the time I got to where I was going, the daylight was already fading. I did the last few blocks attempting to keep watch in every direction. But it wasn't too likely anyone expected I'd return to Liberty Hall.

The house two doors down was unsold and unoccupied. I sneaked into the back yard and onto the snow-covered deck. There was a barbecue there, a big stone one. Its shadow hid me completely, and the elevated height gave me a clear view across the neighbour's yard.

I could see half the kitchen through the patio doors at the side. It was supper time; aproned Sisters were moving about, taking tray after tray into the adjoining room. The quality and quantity of food could only mean a recruitment dinner. There were generally about a dozen guests at these things, I recalled—and we usually managed to recruit at least two or three of them. The thought made me all the more determined to find a way to shut them down.

I watched for over an hour, wriggling about for warmth. The sight of food made me salivate; the last full meal I'd had was the previous night at the hospital. Finally, I saw what I'd been waiting for. The Liberty Circle bus pulled up, and the recruits spilled out to board. Everyone was laughing and singing, sharing "brotherly love". But among the new recruits, I knew, were as many wolves as sheep.

The bus pulled away—and then the floodgates opened. Brothers and Sisters, dozens of them, poured out from Liberty Hall. They started down the street, transforming newly-fallen snow into a hard-packed crust. They went in the direction of the church.

And it hit me: *they'd sold the church to themselves*. With a half-dozen names to work under, it could be accomplished easily enough. They could call themselves whatever they wanted. A different Brother or Sister would represent each side of the "deal". They might even have their own real estate agent!

Knowing this was something, but it wasn't enough evidence in itself. I needed more than just proof of a few harmless lies. I needed to prove beyond a doubt all the harm that they could do. So I stayed where I was, stamping my feet in the cold, and waited and watched some more.

In a few minutes, Liberty Hall began to go dark. We'd always turned off the lights in unused rooms, to save money for "The Cause". Now it was easy to tell that hardly anyone was there. A couple of windows were lit upstairs, in what I'd seen last as the radio room. The rest of the place was blacked right out, except for the kitchen. There, a lone sister toiled at cleanup beneath a tiny fluorescent light. It was a Sister I knew.

I was off that deck and down the alley in about two seconds flat. A chance like this wouldn't come twice, and wouldn't last for long. I slowed down anyway, the closer I got, and looked carefully about. With all that had happened lately, what if they'd posted a guard?

But there was no more time to lose. Without another thought, I opened the gate and strode into the yard. Ahead, light from the patio doors cast their shape onto the snow.

I peered in cautiously. Sister Angie stood at the sink,

scouring the crust from a pan. She worked slowly, a troubled line across her forehead, stopping now and then to flip a chestnut strand from her eyes. She seemed to be alone. I hoped to God she was.

She added the pan to a growing mountain on the counter and went out of the room for more. This was it. I cracked the door open, slipped in sideways, and shut it again soundlessly. I'd hide behind the dining room door and grab her from behind when she came back in.

She came back in, all right, carrying a double armload of dishes. It didn't take a genius to figure out what would happen if I grabbed her now—so I wound up doing nothing. She set the stuff on the counter, turned, and let out a shriek.

"*Shhhh!* Sister Angie, it's me, Brother Corey." As if she couldn't see for herself. "Please, don't call anyone! I only need to talk to you." I approached her quickly, just in case; if she tried yelling for help, I'd smack her. Well, maybe not.

She must have read my mind, because she backed up against the counter and shut up completely while I talked. Then I practically had to give her money to get her speaking at all.

"Please," I urged. "All I'm asking is that you tell the truth. You must have heard them talking about it—about how I didn't kill Ranji. Just tell what you know to the cops. Maybe they can arrange it so you stay anonymous..."

"You—you shouldn't be here," she whispered finally. "Brother Allan warned that we shouldn't talk to you. He said you'd turned against us. If they catch you—"

"Listen to me. Things around here aren't the way

they seem. I think you know that, don't you?"

She shook her head. "No," she whimpered, "I won't listen."

But I made her listen. I told her about the Circle's plans for the Jewish Centre, about what had really happened to Ranji, about what was happening to me. I told her about how they'd changed us at Camp Liberty, how they'd forced us to believe. I told her everything. The whole time she kept shaking her head, and making like she was covering her ears—only I knew she wasn't, not really.

When I finished, she was crying like a baby and saying "no, no, no," over and over again. Then, "Go away, Corey. I'm not supposed to talk to you."

And now I could hear voices, a couple of Brothers descending the stairs. In a moment, I knew, Angie would scream—and I would be a dead man. *I could knock her out*, I thought, but then decided not to. None of this was her fault. Enough people had been hurt already.

"I have to go," I whispered. "I'm not going to hurt you, I just want to get away. I'm sorry if I disturbed you. Please, Angie—just let me go."

I backed to the patio door, pulled it open and stepped outside. Angie stayed where she was, drying her eyes on her apron. But just as I was about to close the door, she whispered across the room: "The church, Corey. They have them at the church. The things they took. They must be going to use them to—" She cut herself off, the other voices too close now to dare continuing.

I slid the door shut and ran, nearly tripping over a cat. I jumped over it, then raced out into the alley.

And stopped.

If she'd told them about me, they'd be out here right away. But if she'd really been trying to help, nothing was going to happen. Either way, I had to know before I did anything—so I stayed in the alley and waited. If they came, I'd be ready to run.

Nothing happened.

So what, I wondered, had Angie been trying to tell me? *The church, Corey. They have them at the church. The things they took...* What things? Their literature? It was possible, I guessed. If they'd convinced the cops they'd sold the place, maybe they'd hidden their brochures there. Or their radio equipment, or flags, or just about anything that might expose them for what they were.

My next course of action pretty much goes without saying. I took a roundabout route to the church, waited until it emptied, then waited a little bit longer. Finally— again—the cold got to be too much. The place was dark now, anyway; I'd watched Allen locking it up. I left the hedge I'd been hiding in.

The long and short of it is, I busted in through a basement window.

For a while I bumped about in the dark, trying to find a switch. Twice I tripped over something stacked on the floor. When I finally got the place lit, I found myself in a miniature classroom. There were stackable chairs along the walls, a blackboard at one end. Probably once it had been used for Sunday school. Now it was used to store things.

I lifted the sheet covering one of the pallets. Oh, yes. They were storing things all right.

Things like guns.

I whisked the cover off the other pallet, not trusting my own vision. This was it. This was the evidence that would prove me innocent and the Liberty Circle guilty. This—I shook my head—this was the loot from the gun store robbery!

Some of the stuff still had shipping labels, complete with the name of the store. I began ripping these off the cartons, stuffing them into my pockets. Then I remembered something Angie had said—or started to. *They must be going to use them to—*

I stood back and stared at the weapons. What could they want with all this? There was enough to stock a small army. I shivered and glanced around at the basement windows. All were covered with paper—except that one black hole through which I'd entered. I'd been here too long, I decided. It was time to leave.

I hesitated just long enough to grab a hunting knife from one of the boxes. It was hard to imagine myself using it, even in self-defence, but I felt better with it in my pocket. I decided to leave through the church—less suspicious if I was spotted. I went to the room's only door and opened it, expecting to find the stairs.

The stairs were there, all right—and the light was already on. At the bottom of the steps, just waiting for me to leave, were Peter Gunnarsson and a pair of skinheads.

Twenty-Six

If only I had moved, things might have been okay. If I'd just slammed the door again and locked myself in that room, I might have been all right. With all those weapons in there with me, no one would dare to enter. But I didn't think that way. I thought instead in those few frozen moments that they would simply call the police. As if they'd want the cops there!

They took me all at once, a skin on either side and Gunnarsson in the middle. I smacked into the concrete floor, my ribs getting bashed again. Then I was up, dragged to my feet, as Gunnarsson brushed off his clothes. Only then did I realize who was holding me on my right.

"You nigger-loving, commie little kike," Chet snarled. "You sonnova bitch. You tried pinning your stinking murder on me. You know what I'm gonna do to you?"

"*Chet.*"

Gunnarsson halted him with a word, but I got the feeling it wouldn't last. There was something in Chet's face other than a sneer—something like anticipation. He seemed to be looking forward to the removal of my head.

"Oh, Jesus..." It was the skinhead on my left, a

scrawny guy with perpetual motion in his Adam's apple. He was staring at the floor, at something that had fallen from an overstuffed pocket. "Oh, Jesus, Mr. Gunnarsson, he's got the slips from the boxes. He knows everything now. If we let him out of here—"

"Shut up, Dwayne." Gunnarsson strode to the door of his "weapons room" and looked in. I could feel a breeze from the busted window, and I felt a surge of hope: if someone had seen me enter, maybe they'd called the cops. But the window was in darkness, facing a tall fence, and that wasn't very likely.

"If your point was to give us trouble," Gunnarsson said, "I think I should tell you you've already succeeded admirably." He walked back toward me slowly. "I've personally been harassed by your Jew-serving nigger cops four times the past week alone. I don't like having my right to worship subjected to police observation. I don't like having to cancel political meetings because someone talked too much. I don't like the kind of attention you've brought us, Corey. I don't like you."

"Sir," said Chet, "you realize we can't let him go now. Even if we take away those slips, the description alone'll get him listened to again."

Gunnarsson regarded me thoughtfully. "We couldn't have that, now, could we, Corey? Not after all the trouble we went to destroying your credibility. In fact, you've destroyed a lot of our good work lately. We can't so much as pass out a leaflet without being observed. All right—hold him, you two. I've got some calls to make." He went up the stairs to the church.

A nervous sensation overtook me as he left. Whatever

he had in store for me, I knew it couldn't be good. But it was nothing compared to the feeling I got when I saw the expression Chet was wearing.

He was leering into my face with such absolute evil that a tremor ran down my back. It struck me just then how I must have been a symbol of everything he hated—or feared. I found myself actually wishing Gunnarsson would return.

"Dwayne," he growled at last, "you still smoke?"

"Yeah," Dwayne replied. "Why?"

"Give me one."

"You don't smoke."

Chet swore. "Just give me one, all right?"

Dwayne hesitated, then let go of me with one of his hands. For a brief fraction of a second, I considered trying to break free. But I was in no shape just then to get away from them both. Not by a long shot.

Chet got the cigarette going, though he hardly knew how to hold it. He watched its blue mist spread into the air. His eyes glittered.

"I never thought," he told me, "that they should have let you into the Circle. I knew you'd be a screw-up. You're weak, that's what you are. You aren't a true Aryan." He released me, forcing Dwayne to hold me by himself.

Then his voice got really quiet, and the flame in his eyes danced higher. "You're gonna pay for the damage you done. I'm gonna make you pay for it good. Hold him, Dwayne. Hold him really tight." And the next thing I saw was the cigarette moving toward me with deliberate slowness.

I turned my head, tried to draw it into my body like a

turtle. Not this, I thought, no way! I kicked and shouted, and they kicked and shouted back until we were all in a heap on the floor. Then they had me good. I was flat on my back, with no way to move a muscle.

"You stupid little bastard," Chet snarled. "Now you got me *really* pissed." And then he made his big mistake: he released my arm, just part of it, to hold me by the hair. I could move my arm below the elbow, and that was all I needed.

The cigarette connected at the side of my neck, and I let out a yowl like a cat. At the same time, my fingers found the handle of the knife in my pocket.

"DAMN IT ALL TO HELL!" Chet roared, and he jumped completely to his feet. I'd only nicked his fingers, but you'd have thought I'd cut off his arm. He raged and he swore, but he didn't come near me again. Dwayne, a little bit quicker, had leapt away from me just in time.

"Hold him!" Chet yelled. "Let him loose again and I'm gonna do you next!"

And stupidly, Dwayne tried to do just that. I was half on my feet, trying to escape to the other room, but the idiot just wouldn't let go. Chet was a worse threat to him than a knife, or so he apparently thought.

It was the pain from the burn that made me do it, that more than anything else. Every shred of fear I had in my mind poured into the hand with the knife. I only connected once, but the blade went into him like a roast. A scream filled the room, and I felt myself break loose.

There were long seconds after that to look at what I'd done. Dwayne lay on the floor clutching his side, bright colour seeping through his fingers. He was screaming and crying, and howling out that he didn't want to die. Worst of all was the look in his eyes, a terror that was absolute. I'd got the wrong guy. I'd got the wrong guy. This wasn't a hater, it was someone who'd been duped—someone like me. And there was the blade in my hand, its blade coated halfway to the handle, scattering droplets like holly berries.

Sickened, I dropped it on the floor. "I'm sorry," I whispered. "I'm sorry…"

Chet was on me in an instant, pummelling me with his fists. Then Gunnarsson came down the stairs and saw, and the world blew away in a tornado of cuffs and blows.

I wasn't out for long. The first thing I became aware of was Chet going through my pockets, muttering as he pulled out the slips. I could hear Gunnarsson, too, hammering something over the broken window in the next room. I couldn't hear Dwayne at all. It occurred to me that maybe I'd killed the guy, and I shivered reflexively. If there really was a hell, I thought, it must have a special spot reserved in it for guys who murder in church. At Christmas, yet.

"Get up, you bastard. I know you're awake." Chet kicked me in the ribs, and I let out another scream. Something was seriously wrong in there—I could feel it. But he dragged me to my feet anyway, and made me stumble toward the stairs. Gunnarsson joined us on the way, killing any hope of escape. But when I saw a trail of blood preceding us, I actually felt relieved. It meant

Dwayne was still alive.

Gunnarsson's Lincoln waited outside. My victim was slouched in the front, holding some rags to his gut. Gunnarsson forced me up to the window.

"Look at that," he said quietly. "Look at what you did, Corey. You incredible little bastard—you tried to off our friend." Then he yanked me by the collar and forced me into the back. Chet got in beside me.

Gunnarsson handed him something in the dark. "Watch him closely this time," he snapped.

"Yessir!" Chet took the gun and turned to me with a grin. He jammed it into my ribs. It was all I could do to keep from screaming again.

Gunnarsson got into the driver's seat and shot a disgusted look at Dwayne. "Hold those rags tight," he told him. "We can't have you losing more blood." But he appeared more concerned about his upholstery than he did about Dwayne's health.

As the car moved into traffic, he began tossing instructions over his shoulder. "You were at Liberty Hall," he told Chet, "when this little nigger-lover broke in. He grabbed a knife from the kitchen and attacked the first person he saw—Dwayne here—who was locked so deeply in prayer, he didn't see him coming. I'll organize the other witnesses myself when I finish up with this." He glanced at me through the rear-view mirror. "Give me forty-five minutes from the time I drop you off."

"How'll I say he got in?"

"Through the patio doors—which he *did*, according to Angie. With luck, the neighbours saw him. I'll take the knife there later, and we can present it as evidence."

He drove on, adding further lies from time to time, until the story seemed airtight. I hardly listened; I was thinking about Angie. Had she told them on her own? Or had they suspected something was wrong, and forced it out of her? I hoped they hadn't hurt her.

And then I thought of myself, and what Gunnarsson might have planned. He seemed calmer now, as if he'd made up his mind about something. *I'll organize the other witnesses when I finish up with this.* Finish up with what? I suddenly felt I was losing control again, more than ever before.

We pulled into a parking lot just off the emergency entrance to some hospital. There, in comparatively dim lighting, the necessary transfer of weapon was made. Chet took Dwayne to the entrance, and Gunnarsson made me move to the front. As we pulled away, I glanced back to see Chet literally carrying Dwayne in.

"I hope he'll be all right," I said. "I never meant—"

"It won't matter to you one way or another," Gunnarsson growled. He eased the car down a darkened, tree-lined avenue, in the direction of the river. Suddenly he laughed. "You're stupid. You know that, Corey? You're really, really stupid. I just thought you should know that before you die."

"There's people that know about me. I've been to the police. They're going to be wondering where I am."

"Sure," he said, not buying any of it. "Face it, kid, you've wasted yourself. Nothing you've done will stop us. The Liberty Circle will continue to grow, just as fast as ever. We'll spread to other cities. We'll take over this province, this country, the whole goddamned continent.

Aryan North America. Maybe we'll dig you up and put your carcass on display, as a warning to Jewish sympathizers. You'll be quite the martyr for them."

I stared at him, more in fascination than fear. *Spread to other cities?* Wasn't it supposed to be a national thing already?

He glanced at me sideways. "Think I'm pretty evil, don't you? Well, I'm not. All I want, Corey—all I've ever wanted—is for the world to live in peace. God has given me a mission in life, and I intend to carry it out. Aryans are the true Israelites, the true chosen people of the Lord. We must conquer the lower races. Ruling the world is our destiny. You know it as well as I, whether you want to admit it or not.

"And my vision is coming true. And when we're there, Corey, when we've taken even this one small corner of the planet, the Liberty Circle will come out from the shadows and operate the way it should—in the light of day. No one then will dare to question my authority. No one will stand against us. The New Reich will stand forever!"

A cold terror came over me as he spoke—that sense of something waiting to be known. It was more than the realization that the guy was completely unhinged. That was scary enough—but there was something else as well, something about the way he was talking. And then I knew what it was.

"You!" I blurted. "*You're* the one! The Leader!"

He looked at me in surprise, then tossed back his head and laughed. The car swerved dangerously as he did, nearly hitting the safety rail that runs along River Road. He hardly seemed to care.

"You really like knowing things you're not supposed to. It's too bad you're not on our side—that inquisitiveness could have come in handy. Well, Corey, I'll tell you—yes, I am the great Leader, the Saviour of the Aryan race. And the Liberty Circle is entirely my own creation. There's no harm in telling you now. I'm the last person you'll ever talk to."

"You can't hide it forever," I snapped. "Sooner or later, someone in the Circle will find out who you are." Saturated as I was with fear, I was feeling a little reckless. Nothing I would say now could possibly make things worse. We were travelling down an isolated stretch now, between deserted warehouses and the river valley. We couldn't have far to go.

Gunnarsson waved his hand, the one with the gun. "Julie and Allan already know. And Palmer, my old associate from my days with the Moonies. But what difference will it make when my followers worship the ground I walk on? I could reveal myself as the Leader tomorrow, and the Liberty Circle would carry on. I could convince my faithful followers that the world was a cube if I wanted.

"Not that I would want to, of course. I only want the world to know the truth. The holocaust, for example— can you actually prove that all those 'survivors' aren't lying? Can anyone today, really?

"I've got a story to tell, my little friend. And whether you like it or not, there are people out there who'll listen. Call them nuts if you like, or out of touch with reality. But they're always going to be there."

He's right, I realized. *The worst part of all is he's right.*

The warehouses were getting fewer and farther between, alternating with stretches of unused land. Wherever we were headed, we were bound to get there soon. I could do something now, or give up the chance forever.

So when Gunnarsson slowed the car to guide it around a bend, I grabbed the door handle and turned. The next thing I saw was a fist headed for my face. And that's the last thing I saw for a while.

Twenty-Seven

T he taste of blood in my mouth. My body cold, colder than anything ever. Hands and feet numb. Try to move, even my fingers, but can't. He's taken me somewhere. He's left me here to freeze.

But...voices. One of them his.

"One hundred dollars. Will that be enough to keep your mouth shut?"

"Ya don't have to do that, sir. I'll do it for the Cause."

"Then think of this as insurance. Oh, and Fred?"

"Yeah?"

"You know what we'd do to you if your mouth ever got unzipped."

There was a laugh, the kind of laugh you'd pin on a small-time hood. "Ya'd prob'ly slit my freakin' throat. Don't worry."

"As long as we understand each other."

I heard footsteps walking away and a long stretch of silence after that. Somewhere in my brain, a circuit flickered finally to life. *They're gone*, I realized, *they're gone and I've got to MOVE*. I tried it again, and this time my body jerked upright. Then the car door opened, a light dazzled my eyes, and Gunnarsson yanked me out.

"Going somewhere?"

He pushed me forward into the dark, where I promptly fell to the ground. Hardly anything was working: my limbs and joints were frozen.

"*Move*, damn you!" Gunnarsson lifted me to my feet and half-dragged me through a break in a fence. A building appeared, reaching into the blackened sky—a high rise construction site. The only sign of human presence was the clattering of some factory's night shift, far away.

"Where are we going?" I asked.

"Shut up." He forced me through a doorless entrance, guided only by his flashlight. Twice more I fell before he found a staircase. The gun jabbed into my back. "Up the stairs."

I tried the first step, but my body wouldn't respond. My leg went off in an unnatural direction, and I careened to the concrete floor.

"Get up," Gunnarsson snapped. "Get up, you little bastard, or I'll blow you away right here." He held the gun to my temple.

Trembling, I tried to stand but couldn't. What the cold hadn't accomplished, the paralysis of fear finished off. I was going to die. It didn't matter where.

"Please," I gasped, "I won't tell anyone about Ranji. I promise you. I only want to live."

He laughed. "Really, now? Well, that's a very generous offer, Corey." He reached into his jacket pocket and produced a folded sheet and a pen. He wiped them carefully with a gloved hand and tossed them down the step before me.

"Pick it up," he ordered. "Write what I tell you to."

It took three tries just to pick up the pen, and then naturally I could hardly use it. I copied what he said. It wasn't until the words were on paper that their meaning sank into my head: *I'm sorry for this. It's better it ends this way.—Corey C.*

I dropped the pen on the step and worked to hold back the tears. "Don't do this," I whispered.

But he picked up the note and pen and stuffed them into my pocket. Next he picked *me* up and began labouring up the stairwell. I offered no resistance. I didn't have any left.

I thought how every battle I'd ever fought, every skill I'd ever learned, everything I'd done in life, had led me here—to die this night at the hands of a fanatic. I was a joke, a great big cosmic joke. I bet the gods were having a ball.

I thought of Mom and Dad and Marty. I wondered if they'd be sorry.

That cut through whatever defences I had left, and I cried out loud like a baby. And through the water in my eyes, I saw spray-painted floor numbers slipping by: seven...eight...nine...

A breeze touched my face. We were at the top, at what must have been the twelfth or thirteenth floor. A construction crane loomed above us, black against blacker sky. Almost there.

I wondered if heaven or hell really existed.

Gunnarsson set me down. We were ten feet away from the edge, and something in my brain was already screaming. There was no retaining wall here, nothing to prevent you from walking right off. If hell was like this, I didn't want to die. I didn't want to die. Oh, Jesus...

The world seemed suddenly to tilt, and I threw myself back against a giant spool of cable. One strong wind, that's all it would take, and we'd both be swept to our deaths. I could feel my heart beneath my jacket, beating with all of its might. I didn't want to die, all right, but especially *not like this!*

Another taunting laugh. "You don't like heights, much, do you? Hmm?" In the flashlight's dim glow, I saw Gunnarsson putting away his gun. For maybe two seconds, I was puzzled. Then I caught the look in his eye.

He swung in the uncertain light, but I rolled away just in time. There was a crack! and a satisfying scream as he smashed his hand on the spool. The tiny gain in freedom sparked me into action. Once more I tried to stand, and once more I crumpled to my knees. I settled for that, and began crawling to where I imagined the stairs to be. Then I heard a click.

"If I pull this trigger," Gunnarsson said, "you're as dead as dead can be. If, on the other hand, you oblige me by going over the edge, there is the slightest chance you'll survive."

He strode painfully toward me, his right hand useless at his side. The gun was in his left.

I shook my head. "You're crazy," I gasped. "You're crazy."

"Yes. Aren't I, though?" He waved the gun in the air. "Get up. Right now, Corey, or I'll blast you."

Except I suddenly realized he wouldn't. If he'd been going to shoot me, he would have done so by now. He could have stuffed me into the trunk, buried me out in the country, and no one would know the difference. Besides, there was the note he'd had me write.

It had to look like suicide.

I reached up and grabbed the gun and started screaming all at once. He swore and kicked, but didn't try to fire. It turned into a wrestling match—me half frozen and him with a busted hand. We rolled closer to the edge.

"Help!" That's all I got out before a fist slammed into my gut. I nearly went over right there, but managed to grab hold of his jacket. After that, I hung on for life—literally—while he did his best to shake me loose. Again and again he tried heaving me over, and again and again I resisted. My fear of heights went forgotten, buried in the battle to survive.

Suddenly I gained the upper hand, nearly pitching him over. That's when he changed his mind. With all the strength he had, he recovered, and sent us rolling away from the edge. Then he was up, standing above me, the gun somehow still in his hand. His eyes blazed like the eyes of Satan.

"Fine," he said. "Have it your way."

He aimed the gun.

And for the first time since collapsing at the bottom of the stairs, I was able to move my legs. With a final reserve of energy, I kicked reflexively, up and out. When I connected, there was an explosion.

We watched the gun together, as it tumbled across the roof. It landed in a darkened doorway. *Wrong way*, I thought, *wrong way*. Why couldn't it go over the edge?

Gunnarsson scrambled after it, laughing. He knew I could no longer rise. He was at that doorway in seconds—but then skidded to a stop. He teetered for a moment at the edge of the shadows, waving his arms for balance. And then he pitched forward, vanishing into the dark, and I realized what had happened.

I rolled on my side and screamed, my hands cupped over my ears. I screamed and screamed and didn't stop once until long after I knew he'd hit the bottom of the shaft.

Twenty-Eight

I don't remember much about what happened after that."

Mrs. Watkins looks back at me across the shadows of the room, her eyes misted with concern. It's getting late in the afternoon now, but neither of us reaches for a lamp. A plane drones by outside, and it's so quiet I can actually hear it. It's always quiet here in the suburbs, a zillion miles from the city's core.

"What *do* you remember?" she asks me now. "I don't mean to pry..."

"I know I lay there forever before the cops finally showed. I was pretty well frozen by then, and curled up into a little ball. They straightened me out enough to get the cuffs on. They cuffed me, right? The guy he'd been trying to kill. But then, I guess they gotta do that, till they know what all the facts are."

"Anything else?"

"Just bits and pieces. The ride in the ambulance, strapped face down so they could keep the cuffs on. Going through the doors at emergency. Hearing the cops catch hell for treating me like that. I had frostbite, you know."

"I know. I'm sorry."

I look at her again, and I can see she really is sorry. I've been sitting here telling my story, and she hasn't asked once about names or dates or anything. Only about me. That's gotta be a first, ever since this thing blew open. But then, she isn't a cop.

Mrs. Watkins is from Family Services, and she's dropped by today to check on how I'm doing. See, I live with a foster family now, nice middle-class people in a nice, middle-class suburb. They're not rich like Lisa's family, but they've got it light years better than mine. I've got the whole set—a foster dad, foster mom, an older foster brother, and a little foster sister who's really all right. They're all all right.

Not that we hit it off completely, right at the start—I think they found me a little bit rough round the edges. But we got used to each other.

"What about the days that followed?" Mrs. W. asks. "It must have been a difficult time."

"Difficult? Hell, yeah, it was difficult."

"Your parents never came to see you? Your brother?"

"Marty's on Neptune. My dad tried seeing me once. I wouldn't let him near me. Sam Winston came, though, practically every day—he's helped me more the past few weeks than Mom or Dad have for a couple of years. Mrs. Haymond came quite a bit, too. Sometimes she brought Hannah. I never saw Neil, though..."

"And the police?"

"Ha. Yeah, they were there all right, every single day. It was just like old times—only *this* time they believed me. Well, after the first day or so, they did. I finally got fed up with them being there all the time, and told them to only come during certain hours."

"What happened then?"

"They ignored me and came anyway. So I refused to even talk to them. I told them I'd answer their questions when their time came up, and that was it. A couple of days like that, and they got the idea."

Mrs. Watkins laughs. "Sounds like you had them pretty well-controlled."

"Yeah. Well, *control* is something I've been working on."

"What about the reporters? You were quite a media hot spot for a while. Were you able to control them as well?"

"Those first couple of days were easy—they weren't allowed anywhere near me. I only found out later what they were saying about me. I've read some of the articles. They were calling me an 'unidentified minor'. And a suspect for murder. But I guess you already know that."

Mrs. Watkins nods, her eyes apologetic. As if it was her fault.

"Anyhow, after that first day or two of police interrogation, someone somewhere realized I was innocent. Without a leader, the Circle was already falling apart. That's when the reporters showed. I have to admit, I sort of liked it at first. It was only after they kept it up a while that it started to get on my nerves. They began asking questions I didn't want to answer, about things the cops had told me not to talk about. They tried to get me confused. I was confused enough already."

"It wasn't all bad," Mrs. Watkins reminds me. "They made you into a bit of a hero, didn't they? And by rallying public support against the Liberty Circle, they may even have helped spur the investigation."

"Yeah," I say. "They spurred it, all right."

"The Investigation" is sort of a catchall phrase for me, one that describes everything that happened after the cops began to believe me. For starters, the entire Liberty Circle was *raided*—and I do mean raided, not just visited. Some private homes got the same treatment, and a lot more evidence was found. People got busted, people got away, people turned themselves in. I heard about deprogrammers being hired by parents, kidnappings made of members, even private eyes jumping into the mix. The cops must have gone loopy trying to sort everything out.

The media got even loopier, and the public got involved. Near-hysteria describes it nicely. Demonstrations were held at City Hall, reports were made to the Legislature, desks were thumped in Parliament. Everyone demanded an immediate solution to whatever social ill had sparked the Liberty Circle. We made the networks. We made CNN. The *CTV National News* sent people to find me. That's when Social Services stepped in and got me away from it all.

Mrs. Watkins sits quietly for a moment, and I finally reach over to turn on the light. It's a shiny brass lamp with a turquoise shade, and it matches the living room perfectly. This whole house is nice—sort of homey. I think about my foster parents, who'll be home soon. I think about the meal we'll have, the whole family gathered around the table, and I get sort of a warm feeling inside.

"What about the nightmares?" Mrs. Watkins asks, and the feeling pops like a bubble.

"I'm still having them," I admit in a low voice. "I think I'll be having them a long, long time."

"You dream of the same things?"

"Damn it—you *know* what I dream of!"

"Yes, I suppose I do. I'm so terribly sorry." Hurt, too, from the sounds of it. I didn't mean to snap at her like that.

I apologize, but it's too late for me already; images are crowding into my brain. All I can see is Ranji lying there dead, and Gunnarsson vanishing into blackness, and something worse than that.

"The one I can't get rid of," I say, my voice suddenly wavering, "the thing that sticks in my mind the worst, is the look in his eyes when I knifed him. Dwayne, I mean. The skinhead I stabbed."

Mrs. W. heaves a mighty sigh, as if this is what she's been waiting for. "You were defending yourself, Corey. The police have told you that. Everyone has. Nobody thinks any less of you for it."

"As if that makes it better." I look at her evenly and run my fingers through my hair. "There. I said it. The basic problem here, the reason I'm not as well as I could be. The reason I see a shrink every week. Satisfied?"

"You're just going to have to give yourself more time. And give yourself the luxury of not thinking about it. No one is going to have you charged. That was all decided at the inquest."

She's missed it, of course, she's missed the point entirely. It's got nothing to do with me. It has to do with this guy Dwayne, who got sucked into the Liberty Circle same as I did. He wasn't a natural-born redneck the way Chet or Gunnarsson were—or even, maybe, the way I used to be. He was brainwashed by a cult. But he's the one I got with the knife. It didn't stop him from talking to the cops, though, 'cause that's just what he did for the next three days, lying in the hospital. He confirmed everything I'd told the cops, blew the whole thing wide open. He named names, revealed plans, gave all sorts of details. Mostly, though, he proved my innocence. And then, at the end of those three days, he died. He just died.

They say it was pneumonia, made worse by his weakened state. They say it was complications. They say a lot of things, but no one says the truth: I killed the guy, plain and simple. I didn't mean to, but I did. And that's something I've got to live with for the rest of my life.

I think I killed Gunnarsson, too. Half of me wonders if I really knew what I was doing when I kicked the gun in that direction. I don't know. I feel the guilt, though. I even think sometimes that I killed . Not on purpose, of course, but what if I hadn't tried to rescue him? Or what if I'd acted sooner? What if...?

Mrs. Watkins claps her hands, crashing me back to the present. "That's enough. You're brooding on it, I can tell. Tell me about what's happening now. How are things going for you in school?"

"All right. We'll do that. School is fine—not many people know about me, and I don't get asked about it a lot. That suits me fine."

She smiles. "Any girls?"

A great big, stupid grin slaps itself onto my face. "Well, one," I tell her, and I feel like some little pubescent. "We've gone out a few times. I guess we're getting kind of close."

"Does she know about your past?"

"Yeah. She doesn't care. She doesn't press me, either, if I don't want to talk about it." I pause for a moment, thinking about that. "One of these days, I think, I'll talk about it a lot. I think I could, with her."

"Good. That's good." Mrs. Watkins suddenly frowns. "How do you feel about the trials? In another few weeks, you're going to be going through a lot. You'll be doing a lot of testifying."

I wave a hand. "So I'll do it. At least now I've got people on my side. I'm not looking forward to it, but I guess I'll live."

She scratches a bit in her notebook, then tucks it away in her briefcase. She makes no motion to rise, though, just sits there staring thoughtfully. I get the idea she's not quite through with me yet.

She clears her throat. "I was wondering, Corey...what your hopes are for the future. Are you setting goals for yourself?"

"You know I am. I'm going to be an artist. This summer I'm getting a job, to start saving for college."

"Are you still painting?"

"That's one on the wall behind you."

She gets up to take a look. It's a country landscape, one of the first paintings I've produced living here. "It's a monochrome. I only had a couple of colours of paint. I wish they hadn't hung it. It isn't one of my best."

"This is different from your other stuff, isn't it? More...rural."

"I used a calendar photo."

"Oh." She comes back and sits down. "I was speaking to your parents this week. I understand you and your father haven't always seen eye to eye regarding your future career."

"I suppose I should ask how they're doing."

"Don't you want to know?"

"I guess."

"Well...your father has a new job, a good, steady one, he tells me. He's in sales, now—working at a lumberyard here in the city."

I swallow hard. "And Mom?"

"Alcoholics Anonymous! And, Corey, I do believe she'll get better. I've personally made sure she's getting all the counselling she needs."

"Thank you," I tell her. "Thank you for doing that."

"They've been asking about you. They'd like you to get in touch."

"What for?"

"'What for'?"

We talk it back and forth for a while, until I finally decide to make the call and get it over with. She picks up the phone and dials the number from memory. She speaks a bit first, then hands the receiver to me.

"Corey?" It's Mom, and her voice isn't slurred or tired-sounding. "Oh, Corey, baby, my darling, I've missed you so..."

"Hi, Mom."

"Are you...all right? The police have kept us informed pretty well. I know what you've been through."

I snort. "Mom, you'll never know what I've been through."

"No. Maybe not." She's silent for a bit, then, "I'm getting better, honey. And I'm going to stay that way. I've got you to thank for that."

"Why? Just because I wrote you some note?"

She laughs. "Hardly. No...it was because you dumped it all, Corey. You threw away all that booze before I could get some more...well, I suppose I had a chance to *think*. The booze wouldn't let me, you know. And up to then, the booze had always been there." She laughs again. "Oh, at first I wanted to kill you. I raged around this apartment looking for something to drink, anything at all. I threw things. I probably woke all the neighbours. But then I saw how clean everything was, and I found the food you left.

"So I made some lunch and drank some coffee, then I sat down on the couch and I cried. I cried for an hour at least, and I worried about you. I'd...always worried more about Marty, I guess. He was the irresponsible one, you were the one who could take care of himself. But now I worried. And you know what I did next?

"I picked up the phone and called Alcoholics Anonymous."

I did it, I'm thinking, *I finally did something good*. Without warning, the tears spring up in my eyes, and I'm practically crying once again. It's going okay. It's going okay, and it's going to go that way from now on. It has to.

"Just a minute, honey. Your father would like to talk to you."

Before I can say anything, he's there on the line. "Corey," he says gruffly, "how are you, son?"

"Fine," I tell him coldly, adding *no thanks to you* in my mind.

He starts in on how sorry he is, on how he's changed and all that, and I'm hardly even listening. But then there's a long, long pause. "Corey..." he begins again, and a rush of adrenaline takes me. He's *crying*, for God's sake! My father, Joe Tough-guy, is bawling like a baby over me! So when he starts to speak again, I give him all the ear I've got.

"Corey," he says, "please come home."

I glance at Mrs. Watkins and realize she knows all about this, that the option of returning is open. Home again? *Home?* Someone to take care of me, someone else to worry about me other than myself? I can put myself in their hands again, coast just a little longer before striking out on my own. Watkins stares at me, waiting, and I can sense Dad waiting on the line. And I already know what I'll say. I guess I knew it even before this call.

"I'll think about it," I tell him.

"Son—I really want you home. This is where you be—"

"I said I'll think about it."

Another pause. "All right. Let me speak to Mrs. Watkins."

I pass the phone to her and she speaks for a bit, but I don't even hear what she's saying. *I'm free*, I'm thinking. *This time I am really free.*

She gets off the phone just as I hear my foster parents pull into the drive. She looks at me and smiles. "I think," she says, "you gave the right answer. For now, anyway."

"For now," I agree, and I smile back.

241

There's not much more to talk about today, so she leaves, and I eat supper with my foster family. I'm flying high all through the meal. Everyone notices, but I find it hard to explain. I just feel good, good like I haven't in a while.

After supper I tell them I'd like to go out. They ask me where, and I tell them, and I tell them I'll take the bus. My foster dad won't hear of it. He volunteers to drive.

So "Dad" drives me downtown, and we chat happily the whole way about what the future can hold. I tell him about a dream of mine: to someday fix what's happened. Someday, I know, I'll figure out a way to warn people: it's our own fears that hold us down, that keep us on the street. Not people who are different. *Hatred sucks*—now there's an idea for a leaflet. Yeah. Someday soon I'm gonna do some serious mending.

But it can wait. All of that can wait for the moment.

Right now I've got a friendship to mend.

Phil Campagna was born in Calgary, Alberta, to parents who moved annually. The eldest of five boys, he quickly learned the art of storytelling to ward off mutiny against the sitter—himself. During a five-year stint of small-town living, his storytelling took on the form of writing to ward off his own boredom. This interest led to the publication of his first young adult novel, *The Freedom Run* (Douglas and McIntyre), set in Chile.

After studying computer science at the University of Saskatchewan, Phil is now a programmer and lives in Saskatoon with his wife and his greatest critic, his teenage stepson. *The Liberty Circle* is his first book with Napoleon Publishing.

More Young Adult fiction from
Napoleon Publishing

● ●

TRIAL BY FIRE
Sheila Dalton
Seventeen-year-old Nathan has had a slightly wild past, and when he is accused of the arson in the torching of his girlfriend's house, he must clear his name and solve a mystery which may leave him heartbroken.

ISBN 0-929141-63-6, 216 pp. $8.95 CDN, $7.95 U.S.

THE MINSTREL BOY
Sharon Stewart
Aspiring young rock musician David is thrown back in time in a motorcycle accident to medieval Wales, where he earns respect for his talent, finds conflict and romance and discovers a new path for his life.

ISBN 0-929141-54-7, 176 pp. $8.95 CDN, $7.95 U.S.

BILLY AND THE BEARMAN
David A. Poulsen
Runaway teens Billy Gavin and "Bearman" Redell find they have much in common when they meet in the Alberta wilderness and try to rescue a man from a downed plane. In doing so, they find new strength and self-confidence.

ISBN 0-929141-48-2, 192 pp. $7.95 CDN, $6.95 U.S.